To Mrs Singer

A decade later a belated

Thank you for a wonderful

Thanksgiving — I've

learned Manners since!

Much respect
from Henry's green friend
+ admirer!

Jeremy

Jeremy Gavron

MOON

VIKING

VIKING

Published by the Penguin Group
Penguin Books Ltd, 27 Wrights Lane, London w8 5tz, England
Penguin Books USA Inc., 375 Hudson Street, New York, New York 10014, USA
Penguin Books Australia Ltd, Ringwood, Victoria, Australia
Penguin Books Canada Ltd, 10 Alcorn Avenue, Toronto, Ontario, Canada m4v 3b2
Penguin Books (NZ) Ltd, 182–190 Wairau Road, Auckland 10, New Zealand

Penguin Books Ltd, Registered Offices: Harmondsworth, Middlesex, England

First published 1996
1 3 5 7 9 10 8 6 4 2
First edition

Filmset in 11/14pt Monophoto Sabon
Typeset by Datix International Limited, Bungay, Suffolk

Printed in England by Clays Ltd, St Ives plc

A CIP catalogue record for this book is available from the British Library

ISBN 0–670–86812–4

For Judy

Far back in the impulses to find this story is a story-teller's belief that at times life takes on the shape of art and that the remembered remnants of these moments are largely what we come to mean by life.

NORMAN MACLEAN

UMBRA

In those first years back in England, Africa was often in the news, but I had given up listening to the radio and reading the newspapers. Only a couple of times, when the Lancaster House talks were plastered all over the billboards and, a year or two later, at *Uhuru*, was I unable to prevent my thoughts from drifting back, but they quickly snagged on those final weeks – on the irony of those arguments, so furious and irrelevant.

After that, I was only once caught by surprise, looking up from the papers on my desk a few years further on to follow the Apollo space mission, until watching the blurred grey pictures of those first steps on the moon I suddenly realized why I felt so personally involved, and for a few minutes I found myself hoping that somewhere, half-way around our own world, someone else was also watching.

And then Africa dissolved. The years grew into decades without a backward glance, and it was only when I had grown into my own middle age that the past sprang its ambush, and I was given a second chance with what had gone before.

At the age of eighty, my father died. After the funeral,

a handful of mourners came back to his house for drinks and sandwiches, and when they had gone I was left alone. My future seemed to stretch, day on day, to another such occasion, another burial beneath a rainy sky, so I decided to busy myself by sorting through my father's possessions.

He had kept little. He had never been one to care about mementoes. But his papers were all in order, and that afternoon, looking dutifully through one of his bank files, I came across a reference – to a standing order, to a name that rose up off the dusty page like a ghost. Nothing, I now see, is ever really forgotten; what we lose is the habit of remembering. With that name, the memory of a face began to return, and behind it a hillside, and a sky, and suddenly I was remembering that there was a place where life had been different, where anything had seemed possible, before my world had closed in.

I sat at my father's desk for a while and then I walked over to the window, and looked out at the dull evening that had fallen without my realizing. The sky was too full of cloud and the polluted glow of the city to see beyond it, to find the moon for which I was looking, so I closed my eyes and I searched back and back, until I could feel the warmth of a day long before, could see an old car and its driver taking shape out of the cloud of red dust that enshrouds all our beginnings.

CHAPTER ONE

I was the first to spot Ernest, and later, when he came to be part of our lives, I always thought of him as my discovery, my secret, like the lizards I kept in my pillowcase.

He came bumping down the dirt track that led from the outside world to our house, nestled in a clump of trees on the hillside, at the summit of our farm. The wind behind him was blowing gently, but he was travelling slower still, so that the dust his wheels threw up from the track billowed out ahead of him, like a spinnaker flapping and filling before a boat.

I was sitting on the doorstep, waiting – not for Ernest, but for the vehicle he was driving. Until then, the only car we'd had on the farm was an old pick-up of indeterminate make. It did the job all right, humping up and down the farm, and back and forth to the *dukas*. But this new car was a Chevrolet, an American sedan, a Master de Luxe. I didn't really know what these names meant, but my father pronounced them with the respect he reserved for his sacred phrases: Early Rising, the Great Depression, an Honest Wage for an Honest Day's Work. And when he did so, when he and my mother talked about the Chevrolet, his big, serious face softened into laughter and she blushed like a girl.

He had bought it a few weeks earlier from a farmer named Cartwright, who was selling up and was offering the car cheap on the understanding that he could keep it until he caught his boat back to England. 'The fool,' my father had said that night over supper. 'What does he want to go back there for?' My father never called England 'home', the way other English people did. 'It's nothing but grey skies and men in grey suits, telling you what you can and can't do.'

He had paused here and glowered at my mother, who in the *East African Standard* always turned first to the pages about England. But eventually his glower softened. 'It's for you,' he had said to my mother. 'For all of us. We'll go to the pictures in style.' Then he winked at us, one after the other, and we melted, the two of us together, like butter in the sun.

The Chevrolet straightened up on the flat and came to a halt a few feet in front of me. Slowly the dust sank to the ground. I took in an impression of powerful curves and bottle-green flanks gleaming in the sun, and then my eyes fell on the dark face looking out through the open driver's window. Black faces, African faces, were a part of my landscape, as familiar and unremarkable as thorn trees or the clouds that drifted by overhead. But there was something about this particular face that held my attention. It smiled down at me, its eyes looking directly into mine, and for a moment I felt I was being drawn into a private world, into a magical conspiracy that only I and the owner of this smile would ever be able to understand.

Then a noise behind me broke the spell. I turned and saw my mother emerging from the house. My father was coming too, striding up from the farm buildings, his limp barely noticeable. He led my mother forward with one large hand and laid the other on my head. I felt it wrap around my skull, the blood pulsing along his fingers towards the tips.

'Not bad,' he said, holding my mother close.

'We'll go out for drives, won't we?' she said. 'We'll spend the evening in town?'

'Every night,' my father laughed.

'And see people?'

'Yes,' my father said. 'Yes, yes. Whatever you want.'

This was the power the Chevrolet had promised: to bring us together, my mother's eyes glowing, my father laughing, joined by his strong arms. We stood there for a while in admiration. The car was big and beautiful, with bulging doors and high, small portholes for windows. White-ringed tyres, splattered with pink dust, circled chrome hubcaps, on each of which was written the car's name. At the front, thick chrome whiskers spread out beneath the eyes of the headlights.

'Now,' my father said eventually, reclaiming his hand from my head and withdrawing the other from my mother, and turning to the driver, who had slipped quietly out of the front door of the car. 'Who have we here?'

'Ernest, sir.'

I peered up expectantly, but the driver's eyes were fixed straight ahead and his shoulders were pulled back, at attention. He was dressed in a safari suit, green to match the car. It was cut tight, but he was so skinny that the cloth fell like a plumb line from his shoulders and hips, barely touching his body, as if hung on a wire frame. His neck and arms were as slight as a whip-snake and his face, with its big eyes and receding chin, seemed faintly ludicrous now.

'Good,' my father was saying. 'Your job here will be the same as with Bwana Cartwright. Looking after the car, driving it when necessary, anything else that's needed. Understand?'

'Yes, sir.'

'Now, where's Gatheru?'

The servants had come out from the house, and some of the workers had followed my father up from the dairy. They were standing behind us, talking softly to each other, chirping over the Chevrolet. Gatheru shuffled forward from among them.

'Ah, there you are,' my father said. 'Gatheru, show Ernest to the spare room in the quarters.' He gestured to Ernest. 'You can leave the car here for now.'

'Yes, sir,' Ernest replied.

'Come on, you,' my father said, turning back to me. He seldom called me by name. I was always 'you', or 'this one' when he was talking about me to other people. 'Let's try her out before I have to get back to the farm.'

My father was not a natural farmer. His crops turned purple or sprouted white fur. His cows caught mysterious diseases that shrivelled their udders like apples left out too long in the sun. He was not from these hills: he had grown up by the docks of Portsmouth, where there were no farms, only concrete and the cold grey sea. But

6

he made up for his lack of instinct, for whatever is the farmer's equivalent of green fingers, with hard work and a stubborn streak. If the crops failed, he planted again. If the rains came late, he dug more ditches.

Each morning he was up before dawn supervising the milking, and most evenings the last thing I saw before I went to bed was the back of his head as he settled down to go over the accounts, or read the latest agricultural report. In the afternoons I sometimes accompanied him on his rounds. On an English farm I would help out with the milking and calving and branding and dehorning and delousing, but here, in these hills, the labour was carried out by the African workers, our Kikuyu squatters. The white man's work was supervising and my father saw his job as a daily battle to maintain standards, to keep at bay less puritanical attitudes, as the workers themselves slashed and dug and burned to fend off nature's creeping corruption.

He demanded hard work, but he gave the squatters fair wages, and provided generous plots of land, and he was always ready to help out with their troubles. Sometimes I felt he cared more about the farm and the Africans than he did about my mother and me. He certainly paid them more attention. When I spent my afternoons with him I would wait for half an hour while he talked about how to send a squatter's son to secondary school, and then he would pat me on the back and say, 'Jump in, you', and we would drive on in silence to the next trouble spot.

That afternoon, though, taking the Chevrolet for its test drive, my mother and I luxuriated beside my father on the big leather front seat, and we stayed out so long that by the time we returned he had almost missed the late milking down at the dairy. And that evening, when supper was cleared away, he did not turn to his paper-work. On my way to bed I stopped and peered around the living-room door at him. He was standing by the fire, prodding the smouldering logs into flames. Then he opened the sideboard and took out a bottle of brandy. He held it up and the golden liquid ignited in the light from the fire, and when he tilted the bottle it seemed he was pouring flames into his glass. He cupped them, and swilled them around, and then raised the glass to his lips and took a mouthful of the fire.

By the time my mother had tucked me in, music was playing on the gramophone in the living room. I fell asleep to the sound of pianos tinkling and high, manly voices vibrating gently through the stonework of the house.

The ceasing of the music must have woken me, for the next thing I knew there were footsteps in the corridor, and then my mother's voice, breathy and excited.

'Philip, do you remember –'

'Shhh.'

The floor creaked a few more times and then they were past my room and I heard their bedroom door shut, and lay listening to the wind in the leaves and the distant voices of Africans calling to each other in the night.

The following morning, my mother lingered at the breakfast table, hoping that my father would return from the dairy. She got up several times and peered through the window, clouding it with her breath, until eventually she sighed and told Gatheru to send down tea and sandwiches, and ushered me into the sitting room for my lessons.

We started with maths, but that morning long division seemed to confuse her as much as it did me. We read about kings and queens, one of her favourite subjects, but even this failed to inspire her. Her face had taken on the pale, drawn look that I knew meant she was developing one of her migraines, and eventually she instructed me to carry on reading and retired to her bedroom. I read a couple of lines about one of the Charleses and then laid down the book and tiptoed out of the front door. The Chevrolet was where we'd left it after our drive, under the branches of the big flame tree. Drops of light lay like fallen petals on the red earth around the tyres and Ernest was washing the car's paintwork.

'Ee, *bwana kidogo*,' he said, looking up, a smile flickering for a moment in his eyes. Then he went back to his work and I watched him dipping his cloth into a bucket, his shirt sleeves turned up on his wiry arms. While he washed, he sang softly to himself, a gentle, dreamy tune, unlike anything I had heard other Africans singing. When he had finished, he stood back and admired his work.

'It can dry for a minute,' he said, half to himself. Then he turned round to me. 'You want to steer the wheel?'

I nodded, and watched him take a blanket from the back and fold it over several times, laying it on the driver's seat. He beckoned me forward and I climbed up and sat on the blanket. I was high enough to hold the top of the steering wheel and see out of the windscreen, though my feet dangled several inches above the pedals.

I turned the steering wheel from side to side, and then reached down the shaft and pulled at the lever my father had moved as he drove the previous afternoon.

'That is the gear-stick,' Ernest said. 'It won't move unless the engine is turned on.' He turned the key in the ignition and reached across me with his foot, gently revving the engine. 'It's three speed,' he said, taking my hand and showing me how to change gear. 'And reverse, of course.'

He spoke unhurriedly, with the ponderous musicality that Africans bring to English. But there was something else too, a way of holding on to certain words and then letting them out in a rush of breath, as if he was continually surprised by the beauty and significance of his own speech.

'What's that?' I asked.

'The headlights,' he said. 'And this is the cigarette lighter.' He pushed a knob into the polished dashboard and waited for it to pop back out – and then held it up, and I watched it glow red hot for a second and then quickly fade to an ashy grey: the evening's progress of a wood fire distilled into a moment.

I tried each knob and switch on the dashboard in turn, running my fingers along the chrome and the mock-wood panelling, and examining the dials.

'You want to see the engine?' Ernest asked.

I nodded, and slid out through the open door. He lifted the curved bonnet as if he was flipping apart the jaws of some great metal snake and propped it open. I clambered on to the bumper and looked in. I had seen the pick-up's engine before, and that of our tractor, but

I was hoping for something more extraordinary from the Chevrolet – bejewelled spark plugs perhaps, or pipes throbbing like veins – and I was let down by the clean simplicity. It wasn't even greasy. Everything was painted grey and the modest engine barely filled half the cavity.

'This engine is very powerful,' he said, sensing my disappointment. 'Even a charging *kifaru* will choke on its dust. There are six cylinders under this cover. One day I will take the whole engine apart to show you.'

'Can you do that?'

'Oh, yes, it's easy. You can take it apart, clean it all and put it back together. Better than new.'

He lifted me down and carefully closed the bonnet, wiping off the fingermarks with his rag.

'How old are you?' he asked, looking me over.

'Eight.'

'*Kwele?* Not even as old as this *gari*. What are you going to be when you grow up?'

'A farmer,' I said. 'Or a driver.'

'Me, I'm going to be an engineer,' he said.

'What's that?'

'An engineer is not the one who drives the car. He is not even the one who builds the car. He is the one who designs the car. He dreams the car and then it is made. And not only cars. He makes the world. He makes bridges and great buildings. He can take the bush and turn it into a city. I was going to go to university, but . . .' He stopped and looked down at me, frowning, and for a moment I was frightened by the intensity in his face, by some struggle that had started up inside him.

Then he put his hand on my shoulder, as if to

reassure us both, and drew me closer to him. I breathed in his odour. It was different from the usual African smell of maize porridge and gamy perspiration: sweeter and stronger, as if his sweat was what oozed out when you bit into sugar-cane. 'Do you know which is the tallest building in the world?' he said.

I shook my head.

'The Empire State Building in America. It is 1,472 feet high.'

'How big is that?'

'Almost as big as Mount Kenya,' he laughed. His ears twitched and his nose wrinkled and his eyes were swallowed up by the flesh around them, like white-backed fish diving beneath the waves of a purple sea. He shook with pleasure. I wanted to laugh too, but I was still shy. I didn't know him well enough. So I closed my eyes and imagined a vast building, in the shape of a pyramid, with a million windows lit up like stars in the sky.

The next morning, my mother did not appear for breakfast and her curtains were drawn against the morning sunlight. At the front of the house, the Chevrolet stood unattended in the shade of the flame tree, so I walked on to the back veranda and out into the garden. It was months since the last rains, but my mother had watered the lawn and the flowerbeds through the dry season, and the green grass and red roses and yellow hibiscus and giant antirrhinums and hedges of purple wreath were an oasis of colour against the scorched brown of the hillside, falling away beyond. The farm lay on a solitary finger of land at the outer edge of the highlands. It wasn't the best land in the hills, not like the lush fields above, where, it was said, farming was simply a case of scattering seeds. But maize grew well enough when it rained, and the grass among the rocks kept the cattle fat – and the view was a daily reminder that we were the privileged, living in the clouds, with the gods, while the less fortunate shuffled through the heat and white dust of the plains, far below.

As long as I wore socks and shoes to guard against snakebites, I was allowed to wander wherever I liked on our land, and I set off down to the farm buildings. The milking was over and there were only a few men about. They greeted me with a smile and a *habari*, and then went back to their work. Sometimes, if I stayed around, the men would give me a stick of sugar-cane to chew, or let me try to milk a cow, laughing gently as I pulled at the leathery udders with my weak hands. But when the cows grew restless, they would take over again and I would move on. It was the same all over the farm, with all the Africans. Life slowed down as I approached and started up again when I left.

That morning, I didn't linger. I peered into a couple of the buildings and went on. To the left, down the hillside, were the African huts and *shambas*. Ahead, on a small plateau, stood the church. My father's predecessor, the man who had carved the farm out of the bush, had built this church for his workers, and though my father had no time for religion himself, he continued to maintain it – and paid for a teacher so it could be used as a school for the children during the week. It had a corrugated-iron roof, a cross painted on one white-washed wall, and open doors and windows. The children were learning their alphabet and I stood for a while, listening to them chanting their letters, like the crickets I could never catch but always heard singing together in the grass.

When I got back to the house, my mother had emerged from her bedroom and was sorting through her medical box. Every Tuesday and Friday afternoon she held a clinic for the sick and injured from the farm, and she took this responsibility seriously, like her care of the garden. By the time we had finished lunch, her patients were already gathered on the lawn, and at two o'clock we went out on to the back veranda, where the clinic was held, beneath the bougainvillaea that twisted up the pillars and tumbled down in orange and purple locks above our heads.

My mother's Swahili and Kikuyu did not run to understanding complicated symptoms, and it was my job to translate for her. My mother wiped her pale forehead and blinked the sunshine out of her eyes, and I called up the first patient, a young woman who came forward gingerly from the grass.

My mother's experience of medicine was limited to the months she had worked as a volunteer during the war in the hospital in Worcester where she had met my father, his leg half blown off by shrapnel. Her job had simply been to tend the soldiers, reading to them, keeping them company, sometimes changing their bandages when a nurse was not available. But somehow she had picked up an understanding of medicine, and on these clinic afternoons she was at her most practical: dispensing Phensic and Veno's and Andrews Liver Salt, washing out sores from yaws or tumbu flies, even sewing up wounds and splinting bones. The most serious cases were sent to hospital (if the patient agreed to go), but this was rarely necessary. For malaria, the most common complaint, she had stocks of quinine, and if she did not have what was needed in her medicine box, she improvised. I remember one of the headmen coming to the clinic with an injured back. She gave him an old girdle and he wore it delightedly, outside his shirt, pulled tight over his sinewy belly, until long after the pain in his back had subsided.

'Your father came up while you were out,' she said, running her hand over the woman's belly. 'He says he should be able to take a day off from the farm next week.'

'Are we going out in the Chevrolet?'

'Yes, to Nairobi.'

The patient said something. 'It hurts when her husband lies on her,' I translated.

'Yes, well, tell her perhaps he shouldn't lie on her for a while.' She turned to the woman. '*Toto*,' she smiled. 'Baby.'

These afternoons were my private time with my mother. Between diagnoses, or while she pressed a boil, or felt a leg to make sure the bone was not broken, she spoke to me, or at least talked into the air, and I was there to listen. Mostly her talk was of trivial matters – problems with the servants, new bulbs she had ordered for the garden, stories about the royal family or English society she had read in the *Standard*, the plot of the latest romantic novel she was reading. But that afternoon, stirred perhaps by the music that had played on the gramophone the previous night, her thoughts drifted away from our hills, towards England, back into the past.

'Your father works so hard,' she sighed, 'but what can I do? He's so stubborn. You know, when his mother died he sold everything he couldn't fit into his suitcase and walked down to the docks and bought a ticket on the first boat sailing out of Portsmouth. The first boat! He didn't care where he was going. He might have ended up in China, or Timbuktu.'

The next patient, an old man, had come up on to the terrace and he leaned forward and whispered his complaint to me. 'A beetle crawled into his ear,' I translated. 'He says it is eating his head from the inside.'

But my mother wasn't listening. 'Your grandparents didn't want me to marry him, you know,' she continued. 'Philip was too old, they said, the wrong sort, a docker's son – though his father was a foreman, a manager really. And Africa, what they thought about Africa! But your father was so eager to get back here, I thought he might hobble all the way on his crutches.' She smiled at the memory, and the old man smiled too, impressed at how much serious discussion the beetle in his ear required. 'You should have seen him when he put on his uniform. He was so handsome. We made you on a hot afternoon on the Malvern Hills. It was my first time.'

Sometimes she came out with confidences like this, assuming, I suppose, that I wouldn't understand, which I didn't fully. What I knew of love stopped with the passionate melting of lips and hearts in the romantic potboilers to which she was addicted, and from whose breathless and overwrought pages I had learned to read.

'What did he say?' she asked.

'Who?'

'This *mzee*.'

'Oh, he's got a beetle in his ear.'

She poured oil into the old man's ear and told him to lie on his side, and he went away happily, poking his finger into his ear.

'He told me funny stories and made me laugh,' she murmured, and for a moment I thought she was talking about the old man, but then I realized she was back on the subject of my father. I had heard this story before. She was nineteen years old and would probably have fallen for the first decent man to notice her. My father was ten years older, not much to look at, with his thick limbs and big, bony, severe face, but a wounded officer nonetheless. Perhaps he told her all about the farm in Africa, about its beauty, its solitude, the Africans who lived there. More likely, he said little and she read into his silence her own hopes and dreams. Compared to wartime Worcester, with its rationing and population of women and children and old men, almost anywhere else would have seemed romantic.

She was four months pregnant when they married. Three years later, when the war ended, they sailed for Africa and she found herself alone with an infant, an obsessively hard-working husband and a hundred Africans, few of whom could speak a word of English, on an isolated farm in the middle of nowhere.

'Sometimes,' she said, 'I close my eyes and try to remember England and I can't see anything. I'm not sure I was ever really there. Perhaps it was all a dream.'

Then the next patient came forward, a little girl with worms, or an old man with bleeding gums, and she shook her head free of one dream and turned back to what at times must have seemed like another.

As it turned out, our first expedition in the Chevrolet had to be postponed indefinitely. The rains blew in early and hard, turning the dirt roads to black cotton mud and almost cutting off the farm from the rest of the world. The lorry that usually collected the milk couldn't get nearer than the *dukas*, eight miles away, and the pick-up had to make two runs a day along the muddy track, the chains wrapped around its tyres merely helping it to slide from one black hole to the next.

My father worked harder than ever, coming in late, eating his supper in silence and falling asleep in front of the fire. My mother looked after him, and spent her days wading about in the drowned flowerbeds, propping up limp roses, my lessons apparently forgotten. I didn't mind. I liked the way the clouds emptied their dark bellies and then blew away, letting in the sun to glisten on a sodden, steaming world. The rain seemed to make nature careless. Worms evacuated the flooded soil and flopped everywhere, helpless and half drowned, until the birds picked them off. Big warty toads appeared within hours and were so tame I could scoop them up without any fuss and take them to my room, where I kept them in the far corner from my lizards. I squelched in and out of the house, leaving trails of mud that no one seemed to notice, except Gatheru, who scolded me in Kikuyu and gave me extra slices of cake from the kitchen.

We called Gatheru the Sergeant Major, and in emergencies like this he came into his own. Nothing ever pleased him, but nothing ruffled him either. He made sure there was always dry wood for the fire and hot food coming out of the kitchen, catching a ride in the pick-up every few days to stock up at the *dukas* – a couple of rickety shops, a *hoteli* and a petrol pump, all owned by a family of Indians. He took me with him once, and when the pick-up stuck in the mud, as it did every few hundred yards, he did not get out to help dig planks under the wheels or push, but remained in the passenger seat, the window rolled down, barking out instructions at the muddy dairy crew.

If I felt like company, I went and perched on the counter in the kitchen with Gatheru and Margaret. Apart from their bickering – mutters from Gatheru and the occasional squawk of annoyance from Margaret – there wasn't much talk. It wasn't that they didn't like conversation. I had often overheard Margaret gossiping with the women from the farm, and if Gatheru was not normally so garrulous, I had been kept awake on more than one occasion by his holding forth outside the servants' quarters, his gut bubbling with home-made beer. I grew up to the sound of African voices, chattering and laughing and arguing – but always just around a corner, or behind a wall, or across a patch of scrub. In the house, or when a white person drew near, the voices would fade to silence.

What with my parents, who usually saved their limited discussions for after I had gone to bed, I spent most of my childhood at the edge of things, listening to my own thoughts, or talk I was not supposed to hear, piecing together the world like a forbidden jigsaw, the pieces stolen one by one. Only Ernest was the exception to all this – Ernest, who was another outsider, who failed properly to understand the rules, who talked too much. But I am running ahead of myself, beyond that kitchen, where it was always warm and comforting, Gatheru scolding me gently while Margaret fed me choice titbits straight from the oven.

Day after day the water came down. In a normal wet season, it rained for an hour during the night and another hour in the afternoon, like a tap being opened and closed at regular times. But that year the rain barely stopped and the house never seemed to dry out. A fever went round and only I managed to escape it. Even Gatheru slowed up, and one evening, when Margaret was confined to bed, I went into the kitchen to see what was for supper and found him fast asleep, still on his feet, his wrinkled head resting on his arms on the counter.

It was the same all over the central regions. Every night on the radio we listened to reports of cattle and buses being swept down swollen rivers, of entire villages under three feet of water, of half-mile stretches of road disappearing. It was as if nature was reminding all the people who lived in those highlands that none of us owned the land – we were all just tenants, clinging to precarious layers of soil on shifting seams of rock, there only as long as the wind and the clouds chose to favour us.

The Chevrolet was put away under a canvas sheet in one of the farm buildings and, with every hand needed, Ernest was swallowed up in the activity of the farm. Once or twice I spotted him in the rain and mud, working among the squatters, lugging milk canisters or repairing the wooden fence of a *boma*, and I watched him curiously, the way I watched new additions to my lizard collection, waiting for them to change colour or turn cannibal or perform a trick I had not seen before.

One afternoon I wandered down to the dairy to see if some frog-spawn I had discovered in a cracked water tank had begun to hatch, and almost stumbled on to Ernest. The pick-up, back from a milk run, was parked by the rear door of the dairy, splattered in mud, and from somewhere close by, slightly muffled, I heard Ernest's distinctive singing. I walked around and came across a pair of legs poking out from under the vehicle, the head and body hidden in the muddy shadows. I forgot about the frog-spawn and sat on the side of the tank to watch. After a couple of minutes, Ernest slid out and stood up, his back striped with mud like a honey badger.

'You are here,' he said, smiling, as if he had been expecting me. He lifted something from the roof of the car and handed it to me. It was a tool kit, a row of spanners, wrenches, screwdrivers, pliers, a hammer and even a small hacksaw, laid out neatly on a long strip of black leather, each item held in place by elastic strips. 'You can pass to me,' he said, sliding back under the car. I squatted beside him, handing him the tools as he asked for them, like a nurse assisting a surgeon. 'The second spanner.' 'The big wrench.' 'This pick-up is an *mzee*, a real old man. His joints are so rusty and stiff.' When he was finished, he pulled himself out and climbed into the pick-up, driving it in a circle through the mud.

'It's OK now,' he said. I handed him his tool kit and

he looked at it lovingly before rolling it up. 'Father gave me these tools,' he said dreamily. 'He was a good mechanic. He taught me about engines.' I waited for him to continue, but he did not seem to feel the need to say any more.

Through those rainy weeks, Ernest worked on the farm, and after two or three chance meetings, I took to choosing the paths I wandered along in the hope that I would run into him. One day I came across him when I was carrying a lizard I had just caught, tucked into my shirt, and after that he took to calling me '*bwana mjusi*' – lizard man. 'Ee, *bwana mjusi*,' he would say, stopping for a minute or two to ask me a question, or to tell me something that he thought would interest me: about cars with magical names like Studebakers or Olds- mobiles, or a telescope that could see invisible stars. I was enchanted. He seemed to take such pleasure from being alive, from talking, from knowing things, that even when I didn't understand what he was saying, it was enough simply to listen to the sound of his voice, breathy and melodious.

One day my curiosity got the better of my shyness. 'Are you a Kikuyu?' I asked. Almost all the Africans I knew were Kikuyu, but Ernest was unlike any of them and I thought perhaps he was from some place where all the Africans tended Chevrolets instead of cows and talked like this to English boys.

'In fact,' he said, closing his eyes for a moment, 'I'm half Kikuyu and half Luo.' He opened his eyes again and looked around. Then he whispered, 'I was a love child', and his face wrinkled into a smile.

I blushed, the heat prickling my cheeks. No one apart

from my mother had ever spoken to me as intimately, and when she told me her secrets it was as if she was talking to someone other than me, some imaginary confidante into whose place I had stepped by accident.

'The tractor's broken down,' my father announced, limping into the sitting room, where my mother and I had been driven by the rain to our first maths lesson in days. 'A rotten tree trunk's stuck in the overflow on the lake and without the tractor I can't get it out.' He wiped the rain from his face and slumped down in a chair, water trickling from his sodden clothes on to the floor.

My father often aired his problems like this: we weren't supposed to reply, and if we did he tended to get irritated. He wasn't looking for a discussion, and we didn't know enough about the farm to say anything helpful, but he seemed to need to have us listen while he unburdened himself.

'Will it be all right?' my mother asked quietly.

He glared at her as if somehow she was responsible for the tractor's failure. 'The water's almost at the top of the dam now,' he said. 'I doubt if it will last a couple of hours. The whole bloody thing is likely to go.'

My mother turned back to the maths book, her face impassive. Sometimes I felt she longed for such a disaster, for the whole farm to be washed away into the plains below, so she could abandon these hills and go back to England.

'I've got them trying to pull it out by hand and they're cutting a release channel,' he continued. 'If it goes we won't be able to rebuild until the rains stop and we won't have any water for the dry season.' He glanced impatiently at his watch. 'I was hoping Joshua would be back.' Joshua was one of the *fundis* in the workshop and the usual driver of the pick-up. But he was really a carpenter, and unreliable with engines. The head of the workshop and the farm's mechanic, an Indian, had left a few months earlier to start up his own business with his brothers in town and my father hadn't got round to replacing him. My father looked at his watch and then glanced around the room and frowned at us again, as if he half expected that we had hidden Joshua away.

'Dad,' I said impulsively.

'What?'

'I think Ernest could mend the tractor.'

'Ernest?' He stared at me as if I was talking double Dutch.

'Ernest can take an engine apart and put it back together. He's got his own tools.'

'How do you know this?' My father's eyes narrowed.

'He mended the pick-up,' I said. 'I helped him.' Now that I had my father's attention, I wanted to tell him more, to tell him everything. 'His father taught him to be a mechanic. He wants to be an engineer. That's someone who makes buildings, like the Empire State –'

But my father was no longer listening. 'Yes, I seem to remember that old Cartwright did say something,' he muttered. He looked at me sharply. 'Where is Ernest?'

'I'll find him,' I said, jumping up and running out of the house. I slid and tumbled down the wet path to the farm buildings and the dairy, blinking the rain out of my eyes, and finally found Ernest by the top *boma*. I told him about the tractor and he set off ahead of me to fetch his tools, holding his wiry arms out to the side as he ran, as if he was balancing on a beam. My father was waiting impatiently outside the house when I ran up, breathing heavily, and Ernest appeared out of the rain a moment later, clutching his tool kit.

We found the tractor sitting forlornly on the lip of the rise above the lake, its red torso glowing luminously in the dull grey rain-soaked landscape. My father began to show Ernest what had happened with the tractor, but I paid them no attention. I had looked over the rise and was staring down at the lake below us.

We called it the lake, but it was scarcely more than a big pond. It lay in a bowl, half a mile below the house, ringed on one side by cypress trees. The original owner of the farm had used a team of oxen to haul a few boulders across the bed of the stream in the dry season, and then built up earth walls in a crescent on the lower slope. In the rains the stream filled up the lake and when the dry season set in and the hillside baked and cracked under the sun, the supply watered the cows and irrigated the crops in the fields below.

The lake was one of my favourite spots and I had been exploring its muddy banks only the day before. But now those banks had vanished. The lake I knew had been swallowed up by some bigger body of water whose great brown flanks almost filled the whole valley. The reeds near where I often sat on the bank had disappeared completely and tiny waves, stirred by the wind, were lapping around the trunks of the cypress trees.

In the middle of the dam a dozen men were pulling on a rope attached to something beneath the churning surface of the water, while further away, at the far end, more men were using spades to cut into the edge of the dam, trying to release some of the pressure without weakening the dam wall so much it would give way entirely.

The engine suddenly started up, but immediately it spluttered and died. I turned and saw Ernest sitting on the tractor, his hand on the start-lever, a puff of steam fizzling up from the engine into the rain.

'That's what it's been doing,' my father said.

Ernest nodded and muttered something to himself. He climbed down and laid his tools on the caterpillar tracks, and then stretched himself out, reaching under the red diesel tank. I moved closer, peering in. 'Give me your hand,' he said, and I held my arm forward and let him guide my thumb into an opening on the underside of the tank. I could feel the diesel still coming out, so I pushed my thumb all the way in until it blocked up the hole. Over my shoulder I saw Ernest holding something that looked like a magnet covered in iron filings. He blew sharply and the filings came away. A minute later, he reached down and gently pulled out my thumb and took over.

This time when Ernest started the engine it chugged a couple of times and then roared happily into life.

'Well done, Ernest,' my father cried. 'Good job.' My father waited for Ernest to descend, then climbed up himself and started to manoeuvre the tractor down the hill.

My father was happy now, one muscular arm on the wheel, the other operating the levers, his face streaked manfully with mud and rain. The men brought the rope to meet him, relieved to be vacating their precarious perch on the dam, and attached it to the back of the tractor. From the rise, Ernest and I watched my father push down on the throttle and lean forward, as if he was willing the tractor to find enough strength. The rope tautened and held – and then the tractor shot ahead and tipped forward, and for a moment I thought it was going to overbalance on to its nose, before it settled on to its tracks and came to a stop. I turned to the lake to see the tree trunk, released from the over-flow, bobbing up and down below the dam wall, a single branch at its shoulder swaying from side to side, like the arm of a bashful black monster waving in apology for the trouble it had caused.

Above us the clouds darkened, and the rain beat down even harder, as if in fury that the watery elements of the world had been challenged. But water was now flowing freely from the pipe and running down the hill in the channel. The danger was over. I watched for a while and then turned to see if Ernest was also appreciating what his handiwork had achieved.

But Ernest wasn't even looking at the lake. His eyes, above a faint smile, were glazed over. At the time I thought he was tired out from his work on the tractor, but now I think his eyes were blurred from some deeper excitement. He was twenty years old and poised at the ridge of his own life. It was not the lake that lay below him, or the drenched valley beyond, but a landscape of his own imagining, glittering in the sun, and he was so full of expectation that he could hardly bear to look.

CHAPTER TWO

The rains passed and the sun warmed up the world and dried out the stone walls of the house. Blossoms burst into colour in my mother's flowerbeds, and while we slept at night, flying ants swarmed through the gaps beneath the doors, shedding their wings for us to find in the mornings, a carpet of gossamer flakes that drifted up like snow in the wind at the stroke of a broom.

In that first week or two after his magic with the tractor, I barely saw Ernest. Wherever technical expertise was needed – with the vehicles, the pumps, the generator, the design of the dips – Ernest was called. He had an instinctive understanding of anything made by man, and within days, it seemed, the farm was running more smoothly, the lights were burning brighter, milk was pouring out of the dairy – and the music was even playing more clearly on the gramophone.

Then, one afternoon, my mother sent me to fetch Gatheru from the servants' quarters, and when I went out through the kitchen Ernest was sitting on the step in front of his room. The quarters were a long, white-washed mud-and-wattle building, divided into four rooms. I trotted over to Gatheru's room and called through the door that my mother needed him, and then walked over to Ernest. The rain had slackened off for an hour or two and the last light of the day was softening in the grainy, slate-coloured sky.

'*Habari*,' Ernest said.

'*Mzuri*.'

There was something on his lap, a bundle of wires and bits of metal. 'What's that?' I asked.

'It's not finished,' he replied, offering it to me. I took it and saw it was the beginnings of a car, about eighteen inches long, fashioned out of scraps of tin and wire. It was still only a skeleton but I could see how much care he was taking and I turned it over curiously in my hands. When I gave it back to him, he slipped it through the door behind him into his room. Then he shifted along the step, and I took this as an invitation and sat down beside him, inhaling his sweet, soapy smell and feeling the warmth of his bony hip against mine.

After that, when the afternoon began to dissolve into dusk I would go as usual into the kitchen to collect any titbits from Margaret or Gatheru, and then slip through the back door towards the servants' quarters. If Ernest was in his room, I would knock on his door and call '*hodi*', and he would come out, but usually I would find him already sitting on his doorstep, changed into clean clothes, his face gleaming, picking at his teeth with a sliver of yellow wood or squinting at a book in the fading light.

'Ee, *bwana mjusi*,' he would say, and I would take my place beside him on the step.

Ernest believed fervently in education and before

anything else, his face growing serious, he would ask about my lessons with my mother that day. If I had learned something that was new to him, he would half close his eyes and listen carefully, seeing nothing odd in being educated by an eight-year-old. But more usually I would tell him something that he already knew about, and when I had finished he would take up the subject himself, adding to it like a musician developing a theme, embellishing it, enriching it.

He had a particular talent for mathematics. 'This world is built of numbers,' he liked to say, and on his lips numbers came alive, like juggling balls in the hands of an expert. He would toss the numbers into the air, forming ovals and circles, multiplying and dividing, and as I learned his tricks, his sleight of mind, mathematics became ordered and beautiful. All these years later, I can still perform complicated calculations in my head, though it is only recently that I have remembered where this skill comes from.

One evening, Ernest jumped up. 'Come,' he said, and pushed open his door. I hesitated. I had never been inside his room, but he beckoned me forward and I followed him in. There was no electricity in the quarters, but he lit a lamp and set it down on the table, where it flickered and threw shadows on the walls. The only furniture other than the table was a wooden chair and a soft mattress unrolled on the floor, with two or three blankets folded neatly on top. A couple of boxes stood in one corner and some clothes were piled on a suitcase lying on its side. A small stack of books leaned against the wall. The room had not been whitewashed for some time and bits of mud and stick poked through here and there. Three of the walls were bare, apart from a ragged curtain over a window, but on the fourth Ernest had stuck up several glossy pictures of cars and trains, and a piece of lined paper, with a list written on it. I leaned forward to get a better look. '*1. Keep clothes clean and sewn. 2. Read one hour a day. 3. Practise handwriting . . .*'

'Here, see,' Ernest said, interrupting my reading. He sat me down on the chair and laid a pile of magazines on the bed. Then he handed me the top one and squatted beside me. '*National Geographic* magazine. I've got more than 100. Father gave them to me.'

'He gave you your tools too, didn't he?' I said, pleased for the opportunity to show that I listened to him, that I was an attentive pupil.

'*Ndio.*'

'Where is he now?' I asked.

'Father? He passed away. He gave me these magazines before he died. They were his.'

'Sorry.'

'I think he's happy now. He went home. He is laid to rest in the island where he was born.'

'Where is that?'

'Across the water,' he said with a nod, and I followed the nod in the direction of the lake, assuming that the island must lie somewhere in the hills and plains beyond. 'It was Father who wanted me to become an engineer,' he said after a while. 'He was going to send me to the university on his island.'

He was leaning forward and with his long neck, taut with tendons, and his big eyes and lack of chin, he reminded me of the turtles that swam in the lake.

'He had an old Ford,' he continued. 'He buried his head in that old engine all day. He loved it too much.' He wrinkled his face up. 'In actual fact,' he said, reaching across to the bed, 'I think there are some pictures of the Ford factory . . .'

We began to leaf through the magazines, looking for the article on the Ford factory, but taking any diversions that interested us along the way, and I was so enthralled that it seemed only a moment later, though it must have been at least an hour, that Gatheru was knocking on the door, calling me back from Michigan, or the Milky Way, to a supper of braised lamb and carrots and potatoes.

Until that year, the world beyond the farm had meant the *dukas* and the occasional visit to dusty towns like Nakuru or Thompson's Falls to see the doctor, or shop for shoes, or accompany my father to agricultural shows. Of course, a part of me knew there was more, that the world did not end at these towns, or even at the distant horizon, where the sky seemed to meet the plains. I had looked at the pages of the *Standard*, and read books, and listened to my mother's talk about England and my grandparents and other people and places and times. But it was through Ernest's eyes, and his enthusiasm, that the outside world, or at least the modern world, first began to come into focus, into colour, in all its concrete and steel variety.

Perhaps it was odd that the grandson of a Portsmouth docker should learn about ships and bridges and airports and production lines from the grandson of an African peasant. But Ernest was moved by the grandeur of technology in the way that so many Europeans were moved by the grandeur of nature. It was one of the paradoxes of Africa that as Europeans cut paths into the interior in search of unspoiled wilderness, they passed Africans travelling in the opposite direction, towards the glitter of men's industry and cities.

Once it became clear that the rains had come to an end, my father instructed Ernest to take the Chevrolet out of hibernation and prepare it for the long-awaited family trip down to Nairobi. I appointed myself first assistant mechanic, and as soon as my lessons were over, I dashed outside and climbed up on to the bumper to see what Ernest was doing beneath the bonnet.

'This fellow doesn't like sleeping,' he said. 'He gets a bit clogged up. I've been giving him a good clean-out.' He explained that he had already started up the battery and persuaded the fuel to flow through the gasket into the engine. The innards of the engine were now exposed.

'Look,' he said, showing me what he was doing. 'You brush the plugs to clean them. And you wipe the points with some paper or a clean cloth.'

I sat on the front wing, passing him tools and trying to work out what was connected to what.

'You are going to Nairobi?' he asked.

'Yes.'

'Pass the smallest screwdriver.'

'Have you been there?' I asked.

'So many times. I drove Mr Cartwright there every week.'

'Is it like Detroit?' Detroit was his favourite city. He wanted to go there to see all the car factories.

'Not yet,' he laughed. 'But it is big.' He looked up from the engine and stared out at the hills above us, shimmering in the midday heat. 'When I first came to that place I was only a bit older than you.'

'Did you go to the pictures?' Going to the pictures was one of the main items on our agenda in Nairobi. My father had patted my head happily when he told me this was what we were going to do and I hadn't wanted to spoil his pleasure by asking exactly what the pictures were.

'I was looking for somebody,' he said slowly.

'Did you find him?'

'It's hard to find somebody in such a big place.' He narrowed his eyes for a moment. Then he said, 'Come on, we can change the oil and check the shock absorbers. Knee action, double piston, very nice. After we can give this fellow a good wash.'

The morning of our expedition, I woke with a shiver of excitement. It was still night but I was wide awake, and I got dressed and sat on the edge of my bed until I heard Gatheru go into the kitchen to make the morning tea.

We ate an early breakfast and set off shortly after seven. I knelt on the front seat, between my parents, and waved at Ernest until we climbed over the rise and he was out of sight. Then I sat down, breathing in my mother's perfume. She was wearing a new dress – pale blue with yellow flowers – and she held a matching hat carefully on her lap. She must have ordered the clothes from one of her catalogues, hoping for an occasion such as this. Her face was flushed. My father, his big head almost touching the high roof, seemed like a god. 'So where do you want to go for lunch?' he asked. 'Which picture shall we see?' At that moment I think we all believed it was in his power to deliver any pleasure, to grant us any wish.

The track wasn't wet any more but the sun had dried the mud where the wheels of the pick-up had churned it up into a miniature mountain range, and we bumped and rattled down to the *dukas*, where we filled up with petrol. When we started again, the fuel gauge swung satisfyingly all the way to full, and we were soon cruising along the smoother road below the *dukas*, skirting the edge of the highlands, descending all the time.

For a while I pushed myself up on my palms and watched the scenery rushing by – the pastures sprinkled with cows, the clumps of blue gums, the women bent double beneath bundles of wood, the huts clinging to the steep hills, the buses and lorries lurching towards us. But eventually I grew tired of straining to see out of the high windows and I settled back against the soft leather, content to watch the speedometer trembling towards sixty m.p.h., to feel the warm wind blowing in my face. I didn't need to see where we were going. It was enough that we were on the move, travelling faster than I had ever gone before, speeding into new territory, into a new life, my mother's eyes alight, my father's big hands on the wheel.

'Delamere Avenue,' my father said.

It was hours since we had left home and I had been drifting in and out of a dreamy sleep. We were driving slowly. I stirred myself and took to my knees, and goggled at the new world I saw through the windows.

Buildings rose above the trees towards the clouds, hundreds of cars were stacked diagonally against the divide, and hundreds more people strode along the pavements and across the road. We parked in a space and I climbed out. Even the sun seemed stronger than in the hills, and I felt its power on my cheeks.

'We made good time,' my father said. 'We can go for a stroll before lunch.' He held out an arm chivalrously for my mother and gave me his other hand, and we ambled down the pavement, looking at the shops and offices and people. I had never known my father to stroll before. On the farm he was always striding as fast as his bad leg would permit; but there was a leisure-liness about his movements now, and even his limp was less noticeable.

At first I was almost disappointed at all the cars. I had imagined the Chevrolet was the grandest vehicle in the country. But before long I was examining them all. There were jeeps and trucks and convertibles, as well as saloons like our Chevrolet. They seemed to be painted every shade of the rainbow, and some were even two-tone: brown and white, blue and cream. I took a mental note of their names to tell Ernest later: Chrysler, Humber, Austin Hampshire, Vauxhall Wyvern.

At one shop window my mother lingered, and my father whisked her in and waited patiently while she tried on half a dozen dresses. When she had chosen one, I waited for him to examine the material and question the price. During the Depression he had worked after school in a tailor's shop, to earn extra money for the family, and he considered himself an expert on cloth.

Whenever my mother's catalogue orders arrived, he would pick up the material and rub it between his fore-finger and thumb and shake his head at the price. But today he paid for the dress without a murmur and we walked back out into the sunshine.

After some more strolling and window-shopping – my father giving some coins to a beggar who stretched out a withered limb at us – we arrived at the hotel for lunch. We were shown to a table on a terrace from where we could look out at the people and the cars passing by. Waiters in white jackets with golden but-tons fussed around, and within a moment a tray of cool drinks had arrived. My mother took off her hat and fanned herself, while I sipped at my Vimto, watching the bubbles appear out of nothing.

'Look how pretty the girls are,' my mother sighed.

My father leaned forward and laid his hand over hers. 'Not as pretty as you,' he said. 'I remember that first time I saw you in the hospital. Your hair was pulled back and you had this worried look on your face, but I was dazzled, absolutely dazzled.'

My mother laughed and I looked at her curiously, as if seeing her for the first time. We had seen lots of glamor-ous women on the streets, and there were more now at the tables around us, but with a burst of pride I decided that my mother was the prettiest of all of them.

'I'd just dropped a chamber-pot on the floor,' she said. 'Matron nearly threw me out of the hospital.'

'Well, if I'd known that I might have changed my mind,' my father laughed. 'But I took one look and decided I was going to marry you.'

I had never seen my father like this. He charmed my

mother and entertained us all the way through lunch, spearing pieces of meat and then forgetting to put them in his mouth and waving them in the air on the end of his fork while he spoke.

'I've told you about the bullet in my head, haven't I?' he said suddenly, looking down at me. I shook my head and he took my hand and put my fingers into his hair. There was a hard lump lodged in the skull, the size of a pea. 'The doctor said it had to stay there,' he said bravely. 'Too dangerous to take out.'

A little later he said, 'One chap I knew they had to throw out of the army. Have I told you why?'

'No.'

He looked at me, as if unable to believe he had never told me this story, that it was so long since he had been so playful. 'He had both ears on the same side of his head,' he said. 'His beret kept falling off on parade. Couldn't have that.'

I looked up at him suspiciously until he winked back at me and we all burst out laughing. On that terrace, I understood why my mother had fallen in love with him.

When we had ordered dessert, he disappeared and came back with a *Standard*. I ate my ice-cream while he and my mother looked at the advertisements for the cinemas. There were four in town and all of them had Friday afternoon matinées for up-country families like us, with our long drives home, and I can still remember their names – the Playhouse, the Empire, the Theatre Royal and the Capitol.

GREAT EXPECTATIONS was written in large letters over the entrance to the cinema. My father bought the tickets, and when we had been shown to our velvet seats, I looked around at the curtains and the mouldings and high ceilings and breathed in the exotic scent of perfume and stale sweat and cigarettes. Then the curtains parted and the picture began, and from the moment that Pip ran across the marshes, past the gallows, I was transfixed. At the end I had to shake myself to remember that I was not Pip and that the woman beside me was my mother and not Mrs Joe or Miss Haversham.

The car was warm from the day's sun and I snuggled happily against my mother. Climbing into the highlands, we kept pace with the descent of the sun for a while, but eventually the last red gashes disappeared from the sky. I wanted to stay awake, to keep the day alive, but my mother's lap was too soft and the rhythm of the car too soothing, and the next thing I knew my mother was helping me out of the car and guiding me down the corridor of our house to my bed.

That July I turned nine years old. On the afternoon of my birthday, my father came back from the farm early and Gatheru brought in a chocolate cake that Margaret had baked, with nine candles on it. I blew them out and made a wish that the Chevrolet's magic would last for ever.

Since our inaugural trip to Nairobi, we had been out in the car several times, and my parents had even attended a farmers' dinner in Nakuru. A new confidence had unfurled in my mother and I watched her handling my father with smiles and raised eyebrows. Though he still worked from dawn until dusk most days, he seemed to have accepted that he could enjoy an occasional day of leisure, that there were pleasures beyond the turn of the plough in the earth and the ripe smell of cow's milk fresh from the udder. Sometimes when my mother walked past him, he reached up and brushed his hand against her back. And more often now, when I went to bed, I heard music playing on the gramophone.

'Well, happy birthday,' my father said, when I had finished unwrapping my presents. 'Nine years old.' He stressed each word and looked at my mother.

'Have some cake,' my mother said, passing a slice to my father. 'He's still only a boy.'

'He can't stay at home for ever,' my father replied. Then he turned to me. 'What do you think?' he asked. 'Do you want to go to school?'

I looked towards my mother. There was no European school close enough for me to attend as a day boy, and she had always refused to send me to boarding school. From time to time my father tried to change her mind, reminding her of my age, or worrying her with talk of school inspectors, but she always resisted him and he had never pressed her too hard. He understood, I suppose, that if I was sent away she would require more from him than he was capable of giving. But now my mother merely smiled at me and said, 'Would you like another piece of cake?'

'Well?' my father asked.

I shrugged and took a big mouthful of my cake, hoping the talk would wash over me. When Gatheru came in to clear away the tea, I asked permission to leave and slipped through the kitchen, where I found Ernest on his step, darning a tear in one of his shirts.

I sat down beside him. 'It's my birthday,' I said eventually.

'*Ndio.*' We sat there for a while, and then he took something from behind him and gave it to me. It was the model car, but it was finished now, and I saw immediately that it was a miniature version of the Chevrolet. It was beautiful. Every detail was perfect: the white-walled tyres, the chrome grille, the number plate, even the steering wheel and gear-stick protruding from it. The doors all opened and inside the bonnet was a tiny engine, with a removable cover. Somehow he had managed to find paint the same colour as our Chevrolet.

'I love it, Ernest,' I whispered.

I could feel strange sensations in my belly and throat, and my head was pounding. I wasn't sure whether I was happy or sad. Eventually, I said, 'I'm going to have to go to school.'

'Good,' he replied.

'I like it here.'

'You have to study. Even me, I'm going to send off for information about studying engineering.

'At the university?'

'Yes.'

'Does that mean you will be going away?'

He frowned and peered out into the courtyard, and I followed his eyes, searching for any answers that might be hidden there in the thickening darkness. Things were changing all around us, all the time. Seeds were falling from trees and taking root every day. Unseen water tables were rising and falling under the soil. The Chevrolet had brought Ernest to the farm and brought my parents together. But there were other forces, other influences, acting upon us, and any day the hillside might shift, the whole world might be transformed.

A few days later, running back to the house, I saw a strange car, a brown Land Rover, sitting in the driveway. I trotted inside to investigate, but something in the voice drifting through the half-open door of the living room stopped me in my tracks.

'Nothing to worry too much about, a couple of cows here and there, the fire in old Glen Rogers's barn, but as I said, the way he farms that's as likely to be carelessness as anything.' The voice was low and relaxed, almost a drawl.

'I'll keep my eyes open,' my father said.

'Yes. And ears, I suggest. Well, thanks for the drink, old man. I'd better be going. Lots to do, you know.'

'Yes, yes, of course.'

I heard them getting up and I retreated back out into the sunshine. A moment later, the front door opened. The guest was shorter by half a foot than my father, and the front of his head was a mottled pink where his receding hair had exposed his skin to the sun. But he carried himself with the same easy confidence that I had heard in his speech. Next to him, my father seemed big and clumsy.

'By the way, we're having a little do on Sunday to introduce some new arrivals. They've taken on that empty farm at Lolongani. Apparently she's some distant cousin of Janey's. Do come along if you like. It will give us all a chance to talk some more about this nonsense. All of you, of course. My boy's about the same age as yours.'

'I'll have to –'

'Good, good, that's fixed. Noon all right?'

'Fine.'

'See you then.'

He held up his hand as he drove away. After the Land Rover had disappeared my father continued to stare out into the distance, his big face impassive. Then he shivered, despite the heat, and looked down at me with a flicker of resignation.

'Well,' he said, 'your mother will be pleased.'

The following Sunday we drove over to the Hadleys. They were the wealthiest farmers in the region, with land that could have swallowed ours several times over and a big two-storey house that seemed like a mansion. A great lawn ran down to a stream at the bottom and gave way to a high stone wall on one side. Two or three dozen people were already there, standing in the shade of a jacaranda tree, or sitting on white chairs at tables covered with white cloths. Africans in starched white uniforms were walking around, serving drinks and food.

My mother had become a little nervous in the car, but Mrs Hadley introduced her to a gathering of men and women, and before long she was talking away happily, while I stood behind her skirt, peering out at the people. The centre of attention in our group were a chubby couple and their daughter, who looked a year or two younger than me. These were the guests of honour, the newly arrived family, just out from England to start a new life in these highlands. Their faces were eager and full of expectation.

Suddenly, across the empty lawn, a gang of children appeared. They were running, chasing or following the boy at the front, and every time he swerved they swerved too, so that they took on the appearance of a flock of birds – one of the swarms of queleas that sometimes raided our crops. They swooped and turned and then the boy at the front came straight for me.

'I'm Derek,' he said, sliding to a halt. There was no doubting the family connection. He was like a miniature version of his father, Mr Hadley. 'Are you coming?'

'Go on,' my mother said, pushing me out from behind her legs, and after a moment's hesitation I peeled off from the group of adults and ran with the flock of children, turning and twisting with them until we passed through an opening in the wall and entered another part of the garden.

The gang stopped. There were eight, including me. Two were girls and the rest were boys. Derek was not the biggest, but he was clearly in charge. He turned to me and looked me up and down, one hand on his hip as I had seen his father stand.

'How old are you?'

'Nine.'

'I'll be nine next year. You can be on my side. We're the British. You,' he added, gesturing to the two smallest boys, 'are the Germans. With the girls.'

The smallest of the boys, who could not have been more than five years old, started to whimper. 'I want to be a British.'

'All right,' Derek said, turning to another boy. 'You'd better be a German. You can be Rommel if you want.'

The boy shrugged, and then Derek told the Germans to go to ground anywhere in the walled garden. They could use any camouflage they liked. It was our job to find them. We would count to sixty.

We found the two girls and the small boy almost immediately. They had simply walked around a bush and were sitting in its shade. Derek glared at them. 'Typical Germans,' he muttered. It took longer to find Rommel, and when we did, we held his arm behind his back and interrogated him until he admitted he really was Rommel.

Next it was our turn to hide. Derek pulled at my shirt and I followed him to the other end of the walled area, where a dirty tarpaulin was draped over a pile of wood. Derek lifted the tarpaulin and we crept beneath it. Inside, it smelled of wet leaves and animal urine.

'Do you live on a farm?' he asked.

'Yes.'

'What school do you go to?'

Although I was a novice in the ways of children, I understood instinctively that I was being tested, that these questions were some form of initiation rite, and it was important that I passed.

'My mother's ill,' I said. 'I have to stay at home to help look after her.'

'She looked all right to me.'

'It's migraines,' I explained, and when this didn't sound enough I improvised. 'She was bitten by a snake, a puff adder. I went to school before.'

'What school?'

'Ernest school.' Each lie seemed to slip out more easily than the last.

'Never heard of it,' Derek said dismissively. 'I've got three weeks left of holiday.'

We crouched a little longer under the tarpaulin, and then Derek said, 'I don't think they'll find us here. We'll wait another minute. Do you like riding horses?'

'Sometimes,' I said. I had only ever sat on a horse once, down at the *dukas*, when I was much younger.

'What about girls?'

'They're all right.'

'I've got two older sisters,' Derek said. 'They are the most horrible buzzards you're ever likely to meet.'

Derek and I suited each other. He was a natural leader, and I knew so little about other boys I was happy to follow, to pay him the homage he demanded. Before we left that afternoon, I had accepted an invitation to come and stay for a few days.

Dreams are infinitely sustainable – and sustaining – until we try to turn them into reality, and then we risk losing everything. It is a choice we all face at some moment in our lives: what we have for what we might have, and in a way how we choose, how we gamble, defines who we are, makes us what we become. The following week Ernest drove me back to the Hadleys. On the way we stopped at the *dukas*, and Ernest took out a sealed envelope from his pocket and looked at it for a moment before climbing down from the car and slipping it into the postbox. It was his letter to the university, asking for information about courses in engineering.

He drove on in silence, his eyes fixed on the road ahead. Even at my young age I understood what a sobering moment it was for him, and his thoughtful mood affected me. By the time we arrived at the Hadleys, I was ready to stay in the car and drive back home with him. I was homesick. But at that moment Derek appeared from the house, strutting forward, not a shudder of doubt in his stride. 'Hi,' he said, and I took my bag and followed him. By the time I remembered to say goodbye to Ernest, he had already turned the car around and was driving away.

Life at the Hadleys was a mixture of formality and adventure. Derek addressed his father as 'Sir', and the one meal we took with the adults was served at a long polished table in a panelled dining room. Derek and I were not expected to speak unless spoken to, though he kept up a running commentary of rolled eyes and pained faces whenever his sisters said anything. When dessert was finished, Mr Hadley jerked his head at us, giving us permission to leave, and we walked to the door and then ran off into the freedom we enjoyed the rest of the time.

We played in the games room and climbed into Derek's tree-house, and rode ponies or ran through the gardens, followed by the Hadleys' pack of dogs. I was a novice at every activity, but Derek didn't seem to mind. He liked telling me what to do and how to do it. I simply obeyed. I wasn't merely learning how to play ping-pong or ride. I was learning how to be a boy, what a boy of my age should say and do.

Sometimes we bumped into Derek's sisters. Anne and Rose were fifteen and sixteen, inhabiting that dusky world between childhood and adulthood, accepted by the grown-ups but not above a bit of bickering with Derek. They might have been twins, and were quite different from Derek: both tall and gangly, like young horses, with waterfalls of fair hair and long, smooth, suntanned calves and forearms they liked to show off, and buck teeth that pushed their lips apart, stopping them from being beautiful but giving them, as I realized years later, succumbing myself, a breathless sexuality. They looked all the time as if they had just been kissed.

'Go away, brat,' they would say to Derek. 'Your little friend can stay. He's nice.'

They used me to annoy Derek, and to try out their flirting and mothering on.

'Do you want to brush my hair?' Anne asked one day, when we found her on the veranda.

'I wouldn't touch your hair,' Derek said.

'I wasn't asking you.'

'You've probably got slugs in it.'

'Oh, shut up, brat.'

'Shut up yourself.'

'Well, do you want to?' she asked me again, holding her head coquettishly on one side.

I wanted to. I was flattered and already a little enamoured. But I felt I should be loyal to Derek. I said, 'You've got slugs in it', and even as I listened to the echo of my own words, Anne's hand came down and caught me hard on the side of my head. I screwed up my face while Derek tugged me away. It wasn't so much the hurt, though my face stung, but the shock, and the shame of realizing that I had overstepped the mark, that it was all right for Derek to be rude to his sisters, but not for me. That incident was something I never forgot, though in my years of forgetting Africa the memory became almost abstract, a sudden surge of shame that the slightest thing might set off. Shaving in the mirror, walking down the street, in conversation, the shock of Anne's hand across my face would return to me, and I would wince and burn.

On the penultimate day of my visit, Mr Hadley announced that a *chui*, a leopard, had taken a goat from one of his squatters and the goat's carcass, half eaten, had been found up a tree at the edge of the cedar woodland on the farm. It was a chance to shoot the leopard. It had probably hidden up deeper in the woods during the day and would return to its kill after dark. A hide was already being constructed, and Derek and I were to be allowed to sit up that evening with Mr Hadley.

We entered the hide after a big tea, Mr Hadley, Derek, myself and an African gunbearer. The hide was no more than a large bush that the gunbearer and his assistants had hollowed out with *pangas*, and thickened around the edges with branches cut from other bushes. We were about fifty yards from the leopard's tree and had a clear view through a gap in the foliage of the trunk rising up to the fork where the dead goat hung. The leopard wasn't likely to come before dusk, so we sat comfortably in the shade of the leaves and branches above us, drinking tea from a flask, watching the shadows lengthen and listening to the birds quieten down as they roosted for the night.

'I shot a *chui* not far from here,' Mr Hadley whispered, as the darkness began to close in. 'Before you two were born. I thought it was a perfect shot, and the *chui* went down like bird a plucked from the sky. But by the time we'd got down from the tree where we'd built the hide, it had upped and gone.' Somewhere out in the woods, a monkey squawked and then others joined in and for a minute or two their conversation took precedence over ours. When they had settled down, Mr Hadley continued. 'The next morning we followed its trail. I'd hit it all right. It was dropping blood. It holed up in a thicket. I went round one side with the bearer while Sam Allen, who was with me, took the other. I was poking about at the edge when the leopard came at me. I didn't even have time to raise my gun before the bugger was on top of me. You've seen the scars where it chewed on my shoulder, Derek. I could smell its breath – bad breath, I can tell you. It was pure luck that Sam made it round so quick.'

'He killed it with one shot, didn't he, Dad?' Derek said.

'Yes, one shot to the head. He's a good shot, Sam. But you know, all I could think about when that cat was on top of me was how beautiful its eyes were. Like emeralds.'

It was night now. There was no moon and even though our eyes were adjusted to the darkness we could make out no more than the vaguest shadows in the blackness. We sat in silence and I listened as hard as I could. I was trembling with excitement. I could not bear the possibility that the leopard would not come. But though the woods were full of noises, monkeys coughing, animals stirring in the dry scrub, owls hooting, none of the sounds belonged to a leopard. As the night deepened and turned cold, I grew weary and I felt my eyelids sinking together.

Uhrrum. Uhrrum. Suddenly I was wide awake. It was a low cough, like a choking man trying to clear his throat of an impediment. Three, four times we heard it, each time a little closer. My sense of time had vanished in the darkness, and it might have been a minute or an hour later when we heard something scratch, very close.

'*Sasa*,' Mr Hadley whispered. The gunbearer turned on the torch and we saw the leopard, illuminated like a pale yellow ghost, its forelegs around the trunk of the tree. It was reaching up to climb. Mr Hadley fired and at first I thought he had missed. The leopard was still clinging to the tree trunk. But slowly it began to topple backwards, and then it fell to the earth, where it lay squirming and shuddering, horribly transformed. Mr Hadley fired again. This time he was taking no chances. At the second shot, the leopard was still.

Mr Hadley and the gunbearer went out, and in the torchlight we saw the gunbearer throw something at the leopard. It hit the cat's hide with a soft thunk. There was no movement. Mr Hadley took a few steps forward and poked at the leopard, before turning and calling to us to come.

Derek and I scrambled out of the bush and ran over to where Mr Hadley stood, holding the torch on the leopard. While we had sat in our hide waiting, I had wanted only for the leopard to come, for Mr Hadley's bullet to strike home. But now, looking down at the leopard in the torchlight, I felt suddenly confused. The creature's eyes were open and staring. The mottled coat was like velvet. I reached down and touched its flank and felt its warmth. The only sign of the bullets was a small rosette of blood on the animal's shoulder.

My mouth was dry, and I felt I was possessed of some piece of knowledge I neither wanted nor understood. In the hours of waiting I had expected something quite different from this, a beginning, an opening out, rather than this end.

To my relief, the problem of my schooling was solved – 'for the time being', my father grudgingly agreed – when my mother discovered that Mrs Wright, the newly arrived woman we had met at the Hadleys', was a schoolteacher. She was tutoring her daughter and another couple of children at home and was happy to take in more pupils. While the roads were dry, their farm was only half an hour's drive away and Ernest could take me over first thing in the mornings and have me home for a late lunch.

I was the only boy, and despite being the oldest, I was behind in some subjects, like French and English grammar. But Mrs Wright was a kindly teacher and once I stopped worrying about the girls and my shortcomings, I enjoyed the learning. And every day I rode there and back in the Chevrolet with Ernest. In Derek's company I was always on my guard, but with Ernest I was utterly at ease. It was impossible to be self-conscious with him, or not to trust him, for he was so trusting and artless. It was as if somehow his experiences had not touched him, had left his innocence, his hope, intact.

Sometimes on these journeys, he would mention his father and the island where he had once hoped to attend university. It was as lush as our highlands, he said, a fertile paradise where even the poorest people lived in stone houses and sent their children to school, where hunger was a thing of the past. 'They don't need to collect wood there,' Ernest told me. 'They just dig up the earth and it burns like the best firewood.'

Once, coming back from the Wrights', I asked him about his mother and he glanced down at me in puzzlement. 'It was too long ago, of course,' he said, as if that explained everything. Sometimes I think he forgot that his own life, which was so familiar to him, was unfamiliar to me. It was as if he was talking about characters in a book he assumed I had read, and when I showed ignorance, or asked an inappropriate question, he was genuinely puzzled. On these occasions, I did not press him. It is only now, in my middle age, that I have become concerned with the past, that I have found this need to go over, to make sense, to come to terms. Back then I was absorbed in the moment. It was enough that I could feel the wind in my face, a lizard wriggling in my pocket. I took what Ernest told me as all I needed to know and if, when I talked to Ernest, I left things unsaid myself, then these were thoughts and fears and questions I did not express even to myself. We feel before we know how to comprehend those feelings, or put them into words.

What I did know, what I valued, was that since Ernest and the Chevrolet had arrived into my life, the circles of talk that had previously excluded me had begun to open up. I was being let in from the outside. Even my father spoke to me more, asking me about the Wrights, talking to me more about the farm. Life was expanding all round. In those weeks, he and my mother held their first dinner party and I was allowed to stay up to welcome the guests. And when the invitation was reciprocated, when my parents drove off to some other farmer's house for dinner, I spent my evening in company too. Margaret cooked *posho* and African stew, Gatheru invited Ernest to join us, and we all sat on the kitchen floor, the door open out to the porch, eating with our fingers, the talk switching between Kikuyu and Swahili and English as if we were inventing a single language that made all of us the same and bound us together.

At the Wrights' I sometimes even found myself at the centre of talk. During Mrs Wright's classes in the living room of her house, Mr Wright would pop his head around the door and ask me to translate what his faltering Swahili and his men's English could not address. He was a cheerful man, but he carried about him a faint air of perplexity. Even when I translated he always seemed to miss the point slightly and I thought of him as a clownish chameleon, eyes swivelling in different directions, never quite getting his colouring right or claiming his insect prey with his tongue.

One morning, he was waiting for me when I arrived. 'Hello, old chap,' he said. 'Could you come and help me talk to the headman.' We walked down to his farm buildings, and on the way he explained that one of his cows had been discovered that morning slashed so badly that he had been forced to shoot it. The men had blamed a leopard, but he was suspicious.

'Tell him I don't believe it was a leopard,' he said, when we met up with the headman.

'It is a leopard,' the headman said.

Mr Wright puffed out his cheeks. 'Tell him that I let them live on my land, that I pay them wages,' he said.

54

'Ask him what they would do if I was not here.' The headman bowed his head and drew a wobbly line in the dust with his toe.

That night I told my father about the cow and his face grew serious. He made me repeat everything I had seen and heard, and the next day he drove me over to the Wrights' himself. It was more than an hour later that I heard the Chevrolet leaving. The next afternoon a police vehicle came to the Wrights', and that week Mr Hadley and a couple of other farmers came over to our farm for a long meeting with my father.

It was around that time that we began to see police vehicles regularly, driving past, or stopped in the road, and a team of African policemen, *askaris*, was posted to the *dukas*. One of the girls stopped coming to Mrs Wright's class. She had been sent to boarding school in Nairobi, Mrs Wright said.

'I think we should postpone Malindi,' I overheard my father say to my mother one evening as I came back through the kitchen from visiting Ernest on his step. A few weeks earlier, my father had arranged to rent a beach-house in Malindi, on the Indian Ocean, for us to stay in for a fortnight's holiday.

'No,' my mother said.

'You heard the radio.'

Then my father saw me at the door and the conversation stopped. Later, over pudding, I asked, 'Are we going to Malindi?'

My father looked at my mother, and she said, 'Well?'

He frowned and then shrugged. 'I suppose we could all do with a holiday.'

At the end of September, Ernest gave the car a complete

overhaul, even installing a radio my father had bought from somewhere, and we set off for my first holiday. I took my usual place in the front, between my parents, while Gatheru and Ernest, who were coming along to shop and cook and look after the Chevrolet, sat in the back.

We took three days getting to the coast, spending one night in Nairobi and another at a camp somewhere on the red plains near the Galana River. I can still hear Gatheru muttering that night about the cooking facilities, while lions grunted in the bush, and can still see the family of giraffes that crossed the track ahead of us the next morning, moving in slow motion, their great necks rippling and swaying like belly-dancers' hips.

While we drove, we listened to the radio, music punctuated by news bulletins. Something was happening in the highlands: headless Africans found on the roads, villages torched at night, cattle mutilated on European farms. According to the radio, terrorists were to blame.

'What are terrorists?' I asked my father as we drove along.

'People who try to get what they want by violence,' my father said quietly. Gatheru and Ernest were sitting in the back.

'What people?'

'Foolish people.'

'What do they want?'

'I'm not sure they know themselves.'

One of the voices on the radio was that of Chief Waruhui, the senior Kikuyu leader, who made calls for calm. The radio said he had been given an MBE in the previous year's Queen's Honours, and I was deeply impressed by this.

But when we reached the coast, my interest in the radio quickly receded. For the first day or two my father went out to sit in the car at night and listen to the main evening news, but soon even he was lulled by the sapping heat and the slow breathing of the sea, rising and falling like the lungs of the world. Away from school, from the troubles of the farm, there was no need to think. Walking along the beach to the dusty town, swimming in the sea, feasting on sweet mangoes and pawpaw, the days slipped into each other. The house we had rented stood atop a small cliff, and while my parents slept through the hot afternoons I liked to sit in the shade of the small gazebo at the cliff's edge, looking out over the vastness of the sea, watching its colour and mood change as the clouds blew past or the sun lit up the tips of the waves like the tails of a million million fish.

One day we drove to Mombasa, and while my parents visited a man my father knew from the war, I went with Ernest down to the docks. Half a dozen massive ships, white decks and funnels rising out of blue and black hulls, were lined up against the land. Bare-chested men were loading bags of cement on to the ship nearest us and I marvelled at how these great metal boxes, held together with lines of giant rivets and loaded down with cement, could float across the same water as the feathery sailing *dhows* that had drifted past the beach at Malindi. The anchor, hanging from the nostrils of the nearest ship, was itself as big as a *dhow* – was big enough, it seemed, to crush our whole house, should the ship by some miracle I could not completely discount glide across the plains and float up through the hills to our farm.

One night, a week or so after we had arrived, I walked out into the garden while Gatheru was cooking supper and found Ernest sitting on the wall, staring at the moon as it rose out of the black sea. I had never seen a moon so big. It was full and perfectly round, and it seemed to hang right above us, as if it had chosen that particular night to watch over our tiny patch of the earth.

'The moon is another world like ours,' Ernest said. 'One day men will go there.'

'Is that true?' I asked.

'Even me, I might go,' he said. 'Even you.'

I looked up at him. He was bathed in moonlight and he was smiling blissfully, as if his words had filled him with a heavenly serenity. Above him the stars were coming out, one by one, like raindrops falling on a pond.

The next day, walking down the main street of Malindi, we stopped on the veranda of a hotel for a drink. 'What do you think of the news?' the manager asked my father. The pink blossom of a frangipani tree shuddered in the breeze.

'What news?'

'You haven't heard? They've killed Chief Waruhui. Shot him on the main road in broad daylight. There's talk of the Governor bringing in a state of emergency.'

CHAPTER THREE

I watched my father and Ernest turning our house into a fortress. They screwed iron bars across the windows and fitted new locks and bolts on every door. A few days after we returned from the coast my father brought home a new employee, Kesi, a Dorobo if I remember rightly, or perhaps a Kamba – but definitely not a Kikuyu. Guards could not be Kikuyu, for it was the Kikuyu they were guarding against. It was the Kikuyu who were the terrorists, the radio told us – the Kikuyu, like Margaret and Gatheru, and all our farm workers.

Kesi had a shiny paunch and arms as sinewy as the string on the bow he carried over his shoulder. For the first few nights he kept us awake with his singing while he patrolled the darkness around the house. But after a week or so the singing stopped and one morning my mother rose early and found Kesi asleep on the veranda.

'Don't be fooled,' my father said. 'He's spent all his life in the bush. He can sleep with one eye open.'

Intrigued by this, the next time I half woke in the night, I forced myself to get up and peer sleepily through the french doors that led out from my bedroom to the veranda. Kesi was curled up, his bow and arrows tucked under his head. His eyes, facing me, were tightly closed. I tapped on the window lightly. Not even one eye opened. I banged more heavily, but Kesi slept on, his gut rising and ebbing peacefully.

I was not worried. I felt the same as Kesi. When the emergency had been declared – a week or so after our return – I had waited for the panic to erupt, as it had with previous emergencies on the farm, when water poured through the roof one rainy season, or when *siafu* got among the chickens. But nothing happened. The trouble, I concluded, was simply another bogeyman: the Trouble, like the Bank, the Depression. Even when, on the way to Mrs Wright's, Ernest and I saw a truckload of armed *askaris* leaping on to the road and running into the bush, I remained unconvinced. They might have been chasing shadows for all I had seen.

The only hard evidence of the Trouble came from the radio. Night after night our transistor pulsed out a litany of poisoned cattle, torched barns and murdered Africans (mostly Christian or 'loyal' Kikuyu). One evening the radio reported the killing of an English farmer and his wife, chopped to death with *pangas* in their living rooms. But I shrugged this off. It could not have happened on our farm, on any farm I could imagine. The radio, I concluded, was talking of some other highlands: a world that was 'like life, but not actually life', as my mother had described the pictures.

Soon even the radio was subsumed into the ordinariness of everyday life. Its news did not affect Margaret's cooking in the kitchen, or my father's work on the farm, or my mother's flowers blooming in the garden. I was back at Mrs Wright's and worrying over French verbs and English grammar and how to finish a story I had started about a man who built a car from mango stones. Only the weather seemed genuinely disturbed. Hot windy days were followed by unseasonal frosts that made the ground crackle under my feet in the mornings.

After a month, I gave up expecting something to happen, and it was at that moment that life sprang an unpleasant surprise – though not the kind of surprise for which I had been waiting. It was a Friday, and that morning my mother had ridden with me to the Wrights', and then carried on with Ernest, the car loaded with blossoms, to a flower show in town. She won a prize, and when they came to pick me up on the way back, she was clutching a cup. Ernest also had a trophy, a letter he had collected in town, the first he had received since coming to the farm. After tea I looked through the kitchen window and saw him sitting on his steps, reading his letter. I pushed open the door and joined him.

'Is that from the university?' I asked, looking at the dense print on the sheets in his hand.

'*Ndio*,' he nodded. 'Application form.'

'What's that?'

'I have to answer many questions.'

'Can you?'

'Oh, yes, but I have to talk to *Mzee*,' he said, meaning my father. 'If he can write me a letter.'

I walked with him to the farm buildings, and when

my father beckoned him into his office, I left them and took the fork down to the *shambas*. Since the Emergency had started I was not supposed to go this far from the house on my own. But the farm had never seemed so peaceful. Even the hot winds had died down. I made my way along the tiny paths between the *shambas* and the mud-and-wattle huts, nodding to the women bent over in the fields, or pounding maize in front of their huts, their children playing in the dust with the chickens and goats, blue smoke rising from the fires. By one hut I stopped to greet a woman roasting white mealie cobs. She gave me a cob and I walked on, biting into the sweet, hot corn and picking the bits out from my teeth. Leaving the *shambas* behind, I passed the ploughed earth of my father's fields, which now lay in dry ridges beneath the sun, and carried on up towards the lake. A little way out, a pied kingfisher hung above the water, shoulders up, beak thrust down, so still that I began to think it was frozen in place. But then it saw something and dived, and came up with a wriggle of silver in its beak.

When I went to see Ernest that evening, his door was closed. I was about to knock when I heard a rustle of paper from inside. He was answering the questions on his application form, so I decided to leave him. At supper I asked my father if he was writing Ernest's letter.

'I'll do what I can,' he said.

'He's going to be an engineer,' I told him happily. 'He's going to build bridges like Isambard Kingdom Brunel and car factories like Henry Ford.'

I looked up at him for approval, but his face was creased into a frown. 'Ernest is a good mechanic,' he said softly. 'A very good mechanic. But it's quite another matter becoming an engineer. The university only takes the very best applicants. And Ernest, well –'

'But, Dad,' I broke in resentfully. 'Ernest *is* the best. He made me the Chevrolet out of scraps. Even the steering wheel works.' This irrefutable proof of Ernest's talents spurred me on. 'He would have gone to university already if his father hadn't passed away. His father was going to send him to university on the island where he came from. The university is very old, like Oxford and Cambridge.'

My father listened carefully. Then he said, 'And Ernest told you this?'

'Yes, he said –'

'Do you know where Oxford and Cambridge are?'

'Yes. No. Ernest said –'

'They are in England,' my father said slowly. 'There's only one university in the whole of East Africa, which is the one Ernest wants to apply to, and that is neither old nor on an island. It has very few places and most of them are taken up by the sons of chiefs.'

'Maybe his father was a chief,' I protested. 'He had his own Ford.'

'Listen, listen,' my father said, more firmly now. 'I'm not doubting that Ernest told you all this. I'm sure Ernest wants to go to university very much, a university like the one he has described to you. But there is no such university.' I looked over at my mother, appealing to her, but she was nodding in agreement with my father. 'If Ernest has convinced you,' my father continued, 'perhaps he has even convinced himself about this university. Sometimes people want things so much they actually start to believe they are true.'

63

I turned from one to the other. Their sympathetic, knowing faces seemed to grow until they filled the whole room and I could see nothing else.

'You've been spending a lot of time with Ernest,' my father said to me eventually. 'When the holidays arrive we'll invite Derek to come and stay for a while.' Then he turned to my mother and said firmly, 'I'm going to see if the school will consider taking him before the new school year.'

My mother made no objection.

Later, after she had tucked me in for the night, my father came and sat on the edge of my bed.

'It's something you'll understand better as you grow up,' he said. 'You can't always have what you want. I wasn't much older than you when the Depression began . . .'

He talked on, but I didn't need to listen. I knew all about the Depression. I knew that my father had grown up in it and that he blamed it for his father losing his job in the docks, and for his parents' early deaths. He regularly invoked the Depression's name like a bogey-man, and when I was younger I had taken this literally and dreamed of a monster with huge eyes and wet, grabbing hands. Even now, though my mother assured me the Depression was over, it still lurked in the shadows of our lives. If my mother spent too much money, if I misbehaved, if a meeting with the bank manager went badly, the Depression was there, breathing heavily behind the curtains, waiting to get us.

'Dad,' I said suddenly. 'Will people ever fly to the moon?'

He stopped whatever he was saying and frowned at

me, shaking his head. 'What funny things you have inside that brain of yours,' he said. 'First they need to invent a plough that won't blunt on stones and a dip that will guarantee cattle don't get ill. Then they can start worrying about flying to the moon.'

All weekend I kept away from Ernest. My father's words had given me a power over my friend I could not relinquish. I had not yet learned how to evade knowledge – to deflect it, ignore it, run from it like a man dodging a legal summons – or that knowledge is not always what it seems. From the window, I watched Ernest working on the Chevrolet. His concentration, his care over detail, which had seemed almost heroic to me, now had an air of futility about it, as if all the world except Ernest realized that the paintwork he washed today would be dirty again tomorrow.

When Monday morning arrived, I could not avoid him any longer. I sat beside him in the car, my eyes on the dashboard, while we drove to Mrs Wright's.

'I haven't seen you,' he said.

I shrugged.

'I've been oiling the car. This fellow gets very dusty in the dry season. I've oiled the hinges and locks. The doors don't squeak like a mouse any more.'

I stared at the dashboard.

'What homework have you been doing?'

'Maths.'

The car bumped around a corner and Ernest slowed to let a cow amble off the road. When we started up again, he said, '*Mzee* is going to write a letter for me.'

I turned slightly and looked at him. There was a faint

smile on his face, and his head, relaxed on his neck, was nodding back and forth with the movement of the car, as if he was keeping time with some tune I could not hear. Suddenly my resentment rose uncontrollably in me.

'Engineering is harder than mechanics,' I said.

'It is true.'

'My father said the university won't take you.' I heard the spite in my voice, and I saw his shoulders tense and his dark brows close in over his eyes.

'It's hard to get a place,' he said. 'But I can try.'

This edge of realism in his voice confused me for a moment. Perhaps I had misunderstood him. Perhaps he realized how slim his chances were, how unlikely his dream. But then I reminded myself of the rest, the island, the other university. I couldn't leave it there. I had to go on, to challenge him. 'It's not true about your father's island, is it?'

He turned to me in surprise. 'It is true,' he said.

'It's not,' I said, louder now, almost shouting. 'There's only one university for Africans and that's not on an island. And it's not like Oxford and Cambridge.'

'But this one was not for Africans,' he said slowly. 'A few can go there. Even me, I would have gone. But most of the students there are the white people, people from the island.'

'The people there are white?'

'Of course.'

'But your father wasn't white.'

'Father?' he laughed. 'Of course he was white, as white as you.'

Until then I had not been certain. I had kept alive the

66

possibility that my father was somehow mistaken. But now I knew that Ernest was making it up, that what my father had said was true. Ernest's face, above me, was dark and utterly African. It was impossible that his father was white. His dreams had enchanted me, but they were just dreams. I turned back to the dashboard and clenched my hands into fists. All I had was what I could see and hear and feel, and I had to hold on to it, to stop anything more from slipping away.

At Mrs Wright's I concentrated on my studies and when we reached home I ran to my room. I finished my homework and then lay on my bed, telling Gatheru I was not hungry when he called me for tea. The afternoon wore on and slowly the light began to drain from the world. It was exactly a month since we had returned from the coast and as I stared out of the window the ghost of a full moon began to rise into the greying sky. I watched it until almost the whole face was visible, and then I quickly turned away – back from the deceiving sky to the ordinary certainties of my room, the house, the smell of supper cooking in the kitchen.

In the following days, the world had a hollow feel to it. My thoughts jangled in my head, and when I rode with Ernest back and forth to Mrs Wright's, our stilted talk echoed around the Chevrolet, tinny and false. My parents seemed unsettled too. One afternoon my father drove back from town with a pair of revolvers he had bought, part of an emergency batch flown out from England. My mother narrowed her eyes when he showed them to her and said nothing. But that night I heard the sound of their strained voices through the bedroom door and I caught the words 'never' and 'home' among my mother's tense whispers. From then on, my father kept his gun with him all the time, in a holster on his waist, or beside him at table, or on the arm of his chair. But he did not treat it lovingly, as Mr Hadley had his rifle, and when I asked if I could hold the gun, he shook his head and told me it wasn't a toy. My mother refused to carry her revolver and after that first evening it did not reappear. Some days later, when both my parents were out of the house, I stole into their room and opened my mother's bedside drawer. The gun was where I had expected, beneath her handkerchiefs. I picked it up and held it in my hand. It was heavier than I had imagined, and cold. It was different from Mr Hadley's rifle, uglier, more threatening. I half expected it to come to life in my hands. But it just lay there, a dull black threat, until I slid it away and closed the drawer.

That same week my father went on the first of many night patrols which Mr Hadley had instigated with other local farmers, under the supervision of the Police Reserve. A car came for him at dusk and dropped him back sometime much later in the night. The next morning, at breakfast, both my parents looked tired, and I guessed that my mother must have waited up for my father. But the following day, while my father had recovered his energies, my mother had worsened. Her face was pale and drawn, and when she tried to eat a piece of bread she grimaced and then disappeared back into her bedroom. She was in bed when I came home from school, and I tiptoed in and asked if she was having a migraine. She shook her head and smiled wanly. A little later, she came out into the garden and walked gingerly down to her flowerbeds. But she soon returned to the house and remained in bed for supper, and throughout the next day.

The doctor was called, and while he attended my mother, my father and I waited in the living room. I was used to my mother's migraines, but this was different. There was an air of uncertainty in the house, as if something that I could not be told about was being decided. When the doctor came to the door and beckoned my father into the bedroom, I felt left out and fed up, and I walked into the garden.

It was a beautiful day. The unstable weather had blown itself out and the long dry season had settled in. Against the shrivelled trees and cracked earth the sky seemed even bigger and bluer than usual. It was hot and I walked slowly, picking up a dry stick and poking about in the bushes and grass as I went. An agama lizard ran across the path and stopped suddenly on a rock, its metallic orange head bobbing frantically up and down. I thought about trying to catch it but dismissed the idea. It was too hot and anyway, I had decided, I was growing out of lizards.

The dry months had sapped the lake, and the water was surrounded by a broad belt of bare dried mud, patterned with spidery cracks. A troop of vervet monkeys had taken up residence in the cypress trees and several were squatting in the shade on the ground. When I approached they shrieked and scuttled up the trunk into the branches. I glowered back at them and sat down on the bank, my knees pulled up to my chest. There was no wind and the lake was as flat and dark as the dining-room table when Gatheru had polished it. I broke off a bit of dry mud beside me and lobbed it a few feet out. The ripples spread across the surface.

I wasn't supposed to set foot in the lake: bilharzia and worms and other diseases lurked in the mud and brown water. But that day I wasn't afraid. I wanted to feel the cold mud oozing between my toes. I felt angry, careless. An idea had come into my head and I couldn't shake it free. For all I cared, sickness could seep into my pores, worms could tunnel into my feet.

I was about to unlace my shoes when I heard footfalls crunching on the path overhead. I looked up and my father waved at me. I turned back to the lake and tossed another piece of dry mud into the water. My father walked up and sat down beside me, pulling his big knees up to his chest too. The monkeys had started hooting again at his arrival, but after a minute or two they quietened down.

'You shouldn't come down here on your own,' he said eventually. 'Not until the Trouble is finished.'

I kept my silence, and he remained beside me, peering out over the lake, as if trying to see what I was looking at, to understand what it was like to be a boy on these banks on this hot day. After a while, he said, 'I've got something to tell you.'

'I know,' I said carelessly. I had worked it out. I had read about it in my mother's books. It was what happened to beautiful, fragile women: they got consumption, pneumonia. I kept my eyes fixed to the front and mustered a tone of resignation. 'Mum's dying,' I said.

'Dying?' He yelped in surprise. 'No, she's not dying,' he said. 'She's going to have a baby.'

Tiny waves were still lapping at the shore in front of

me. Not far away an insect hovered motionless, an inch above the water. Then it twitched and was gone. I tried concentrating on the lake, fixing a point and holding my eyes on it. But my belly was hurting and my face began to burn. I reached up to touch the skin on my cheeks and felt the wetness. My father put his arm around me and I let him pull me into his chest, so I could hide my tears. In all those years, that was the only time I can remember crying, and the only time my father held me like that. When I had caught my breath, he helped me to my feet and we walked gently up the hill, my hand enfolded in his.

My father treated my mother with a tenderness he usually reserved for his prize milkers. He walked up to the house several times a day and stood about awkwardly, getting in everyone's way. Sometimes I would find him simply watching her, a bemused smile on his big face, as if he did not quite understand why he was so affected by what the both of them had done. She was still sickly, but now she had an explanation for her nausea she did not give in to it. She was imbued with a new purpose and fussed about the house, clearing out the spare bedroom, sending off for catalogues. I never found out whether the conception was a mistake or a surprise after years of trying. But it was gratefully received. Counting back, I reckon there must have been a powerful magic in those hot, sultry afternoons at the coast.

To me, the house now seemed like a cocoon, wrapping us all up in its warmth. New life was throbbing in my mother's belly, and in every room, behind every door. The rest of the world – Ernest, the Trouble, what lay outside the walls, beyond the hedge at the bottom of the garden – mattered only in how it related to my mother's condition. When the news spread to the farm workers they brought gifts of sweet potatoes and green bananas. The pregnancy was a good sign. They thought a woman should have eight or ten children, as they did, and had pitied my mother, and worried about the curse of her aridity. Margaret too clucked her approval, and began making some special Kikuyu tea to help my mother with her sickness, and cooking up extra food to make the baby strong and ensure it was a boy.

When Ernest expressed pleasure at the news, I even softened towards him and told him about my lessons, though I let his replies flow over me. Not all his talk was unreliable – much of what he said corresponded to what I learned elsewhere – but I could no longer trust him. His words had lost their magic, their power to enchant me. I no longer felt heady when he juggled with numbers or spun ideas like silk.

But it mattered less to me now. I had something new to wonder at. My mother's body was changing. Her breasts had swollen and her arms and legs were thickening. As Christmas approached her belly began to grow, and she took my hand and held it against her stomach. 'Soon you'll be able to feel it kicking,' she whispered, and I trembled at the thought.

In the excitement, the urgency of getting me into a school seemed to have been forgotten, and with my mother needing peace and quiet, Derek's planned visit was put off. I was secretly relieved. I had worried that there would be nothing to entertain Derek in our little house and garden; and anyway, I no longer needed a friend. My own special companion was being made inside my mother. In the week before Christmas, we drove down to Nairobi for another day out, shopping for maternity clothes, and seeing a film, something starring Ralph Richardson. I remember, because around that time Ralph Richardson was in Nairobi, appearing at the opening of the National Theatre, and there were posters of him up all over town. I was amazed that someone from the pictures existed in real life, could step out of the screen into our own capital. One evening we heard him on the radio, reading the *Hunting of the Snark*. Another evening I remember listening to reports of freezing fogs in England which had killed 200 people. Two hundred! I had never seen that many people. I snuggled against my mother while we listened, relieved that we lived in these secure hills and not in wild, unpredictable England.

One day, in the week before Christmas, I helped my father and a crew of men spell out our surname on the lawn in whitewashed rocks. My mother was out shopping, and when she returned she protested at her spoiled lawn. But a day or two later, when a small plane flew overhead, she followed me into the garden and waved as the plane buzzed us, and then dipped its wings in salute and flew off.

We had a quiet Christmas at home, Margaret cooking turkey and Gatheru bringing in a pudding flaming with my father's brandy. The next day we drove over to the Hadleys for their annual Boxing Day party. I don't think there had been much going out since the Trouble had started and everyone drank quickly, to make up. But the mood wasn't right. People were nervous, were aware of the need to let things out, to have a good time, to laugh off their worries, and the more drink the waiters carried out from the house, the more sober everyone seemed to become – all except one guest, a large, fat man who laughed uproariously at anything anyone said, and then suddenly keeled over and lay unconscious on the grass.

'I hope it's a boy,' Derek said, when I told him about my mother's pregnancy.

'Me too,' I said, though a part of me wanted a girl, like one of Derek's sisters. I watched them showing off their brown arms and walked past them, breathing in their strange, high, intoxicating scent.

'Come on,' Derek said, and we picked our way through the adults, spying on their guns. A woman's handbag lay open on a table, and we peeked inside and saw a pearl handle disappearing into the shadows. Some of the men had revolvers on their hips, or in shoulder holsters hanging in front of their armpits. One or two butts stuck out of pockets. We found a young man sitting on his own under a tree, holding his drink with both hands, a faint line of wet foam on his moustache.

'What kind of gun have you got?' Derek asked.

'Webley thirty-eight,' the man said, coming to life.

'Have you shot any gangsters?'

'Not yet.'

'Let me hold it.'

Obediently, the man drew the revolver from his holster and let Derek weigh it in his hands. He passed it to me. It looked like a larger version of my mother's gun. I gave it back to the man, and he suddenly held it up and pointed it at us. I drew back and he gave a short laugh.

'You have to cock it first,' he said. 'Look, you pull the hammer back with your thumb. See?'

'I know that,' Derek said, raising his eyebrows. Before we left he asked if I wanted to come to stay, but I made some excuse. I wanted to be near my mother. I was waiting for the first kick, the first sign of the new life.

The old year gave way to the new, and the doctor came to check up on my mother. She was still feeling sick, but he said it wouldn't last much longer. I was back at Mrs Wright's for the new term and one day, when Ernest came to collect me, I saw a brown envelope, the top torn off, in his pocket. He asked me how school had been, but when I began to answer him he wasn't listening.

I looked out of the corner of my eye at the envelope. I didn't need to be told what it contained. I could read the university's answer on Ernest's face. His eyes kept opening wide and his Adam's apple throbbed on his throat. He looked more shocked than saddened, as if he had just found a snake in his bed.

'*Pole*, Ernest, *pole*,' I whispered silently. 'Sorry.' Africans said sorry all the time. If you knocked your glass over in a restaurant a waiter would rush over saying '*pole, pole*'. If you dropped something in the street, if someone bumped into you, if they saw you unhappy, they would say sorry, sorry that it happened. I wanted to say sorry aloud to Ernest, to tell him that even if his dream was impossible I was still sorry he couldn't have it. But I was too wary to open myself up to him again. He had betrayed me and I was still angry, still suspicious, as well as sorry.

One evening, towards the middle of January, a jeep pulled up to collect my father for his weekly night patrol. My mother locked the front door after him, and when Margaret and Gatheru were finished clearing up she fastened the kitchen door behind them. When I was ready in bed, she came and sat beside me for a while. 'Perhaps it will be a girl this time,' she said. 'I thought you were going to be a girl because you were so quiet inside. The other women at the hospital all had kickers. But you were curled up in there thinking, listening. That's what I thought. You were the same when you came out. You never made a fuss. You just lay in your cot watching everything happen, taking it all in.' Before she left, she checked the lock on the French door to the veranda, and then I followed her to the door and bolted it behind her before climbing back into bed.

It was long into the night when I woke. The room was in utter darkness and there was no sound from the servants' quarters, or the road. Everything was silent. But I was certain something had woken me. I could hear its echo in my head, like the trace of a light bulb in the moment after it has been turned off. I held my breath, listening as hard as I could, pressing my ear up against the silence until it suddenly shattered, and I was almost propelled from my bed towards the ceiling.

I jerked upright and turned on the light. The room was empty. I scrambled down and looked under the bed. Nothing. The sound had been sharp and short and dissonant. Listening to its reverberations in my head, it seemed to me a parrot had squawked, or someone had banged all the keys of a piano at once, though we didn't have a piano in the house. I put on my dressing gown and pulled back the bolt on the door, peering out into the corridor. To my right, towards the living room and kitchen, all was quiet. But to my left, the door to the spare room hung ajar, and beyond, a soft light was filtering out from the open door to my parents' bedroom. Standing in the light was a figure.

'Dad?' I said, but as the words left my mouth I scolded myself for being so stupid. It couldn't be my father. The man's skin was black, or at least yellow in the lukewarm glow of the artificial light. I said, 'Who are you?'

He turned towards me. His yellow face looked sickly, sallow, damp. Even the whites of his eyes were yellow, as if the brown irises had run into the whites. His upper lip was curled back, and I could see the tops of his teeth beneath the papery sheen of his gums. I squinted at him in the half-light. Although his face was grotesquely distorted, it was still familiar. I was sure he was one of our squatters, though I couldn't work out which one. But what was he doing in the house? So late at night?

Then the spare-room door squeaked and another figure emerged. This one I recognized at once. It was Ernest. I started to say his name, but he thrust the palm of his hand at me and turned down the corridor. He took a pace towards the yellow man and said something in Kikuyu I did not understand, though I picked up the harshness in his voice. The yellow man retreated at this and raised his arm. I saw that in his hand was a *panga*.

Perhaps if I had not recognized the yellow man, I might then have felt fear. But at that moment I realized he was Munyi – the squatter whose wife had given me the maize cob only a few weeks earlier. In fact, I had talked to Munyi himself not too long before, down at the dairy. He was a pleasant man. He looked ill now, though. His face was contorted with pain or fever. That was why he had come to the house – in search of treatment from my mother. He was so sick that he could not wait until the next clinic. It was probably an infection, for I knew from my mother's clinics how quickly these spread through the body. He must have cut himself with the *panga* and had brought it with him to show my mother. She always asked to see what had caused wounds: the nail or knife, or even snake, if it was caught and killed.

Ernest spoke again, and Munyi lifted the *panga* higher. Then his fingers loosened around the handle and the weapon fell to the ground, clattering along the floor. The sound seemed to jerk Munyi out of his trance and he lurched forward, head down, towards Ernest. For a moment I thought he was going to throw his arms around Ernest's waist, but instead he pushed Ernest out of the way and twisted through the door into the spare room.

When Ernest had recovered, he darted after Munyi. I waited a moment and then took a few steps forward and peered into the spare room. Ernest was at the French doors. The night was streaming into the room. There was no sign of Munyi. A wisp of cold air brushed against my face, and I stirred and ran down the corridor, sidestepping the *panga*, which still lay on the floorboards.

'Mum,' I said. She was standing back from her bedroom door, silhouetted by the light behind her. Her shadowed face looked bloodless. In her hand, held limply, was her gun. She was pointing it through the doorway, though the barrel faced down, towards my feet.

'I didn't shoot,' she whispered.

I reached forward and took the gun from her limp hand. I didn't think she should be pointing it at anybody. 'You couldn't have,' I said, looking at it. 'You need to cock it with your thumb first, like this.' She stared down at my hands as I demonstrated. Then she said, 'What are you doing?'

'Showing you how it works.'

'Give it to me, give it to me.' Reluctantly I returned it to her, and as she took it, there was a sound behind me and she lifted it up again, pointing it wildly over my shoulder. I twisted round to see a face, a new face, in the doorway. But it was only Kesi, holding his bow and arrow in one hand, rubbing the sleep from his eyes with the other. He must have slept through the whole business. My mother shivered and lowered the gun, and stumbled back towards the bed.

Now Ernest appeared in the doorway.

'Is Mama all right?' he said softly. He was holding the *panga*. I looked at her, but she was staring wordlessly ahead of her, so I told Ernest that she was.

'Come for one minute,' he said, and I followed him out into the corridor. 'I've checked, there is no one here. We are going out on to the veranda. We will wait there for your father. You lock the door behind us.'

'What if –' I began, but Ernest interrupted me. 'Come,' he said. '*Sasa*.' I frowned at him, but I did what he asked. Then I returned to my mother and sat with her, holding her hand, feeling her trembling beside me, until we heard the drone of the car winding its way unhurriedly down the hillside.

My father took me out on to the lawn and we stood together amid the white stones. 'Your mother is going back to England for a while,' he said.

'To England?'

'For a while.' The words echoed in the hot air. 'She's not well and she needs time away to recover.'

'Is she going to see Grandpa and Grandma?'

'Yes, she'll stay with them.'

'Am I going with her?'

'You are going to go to school. I've talked to them. You can start immediately, next week.'

'Where are you going?'

'I'll be staying here of course.'

The sun on the white stones was almost blinding. I closed my eyes but I still saw the white spots. 'I could stay here with you.'

He reached out and put his hand on my shoulder, man to man. 'It's time you went to proper school,' he said. 'I've said I'll have you there on Tuesday. We'll drive down to Nairobi tomorrow. Your mother is going to spend some time in hospital until she's well enough to travel. We can buy your school uniform there, then I'll drive you up to school.'

'I like it at Mrs Wright's.'

He ignored this. 'Your mother's up for a visit now,' he said eventually. 'Why don't you go and see her?'

It was four days since the break-in and I had not seen my mother in all that time. She was having a very bad migraine, my father had explained on the first day, and

I had not asked after that. The doctor had been several times.

That first morning the police had come by the lorry-load. They had tramped in and out of the house, tracked around the garden, marched about the farm. Munyi was found without trouble, sitting outside his hut, waiting. He had made no attempt to escape. He was driven away, but the police stayed on.

I watched them, bewildered by what had been brought down upon us. The night's events had opened up the farm, had opened up our lives, to the outside world, to these serious-faced policemen. We were no longer deemed able to sort out our problems ourselves. The police had been called in and they were now in charge. It was what they thought that mattered. That day they interviewed the servants, Ernest, my father, even me. When I overheard an officer grilling my father over why the doors into the spare room had not been secured, I realized with dull horror that he believed one of the servants had deliberately left them open – that Margaret and Gatheru were at risk. My father defended them desperately, repeating, to the sergeant's disgust, that we were careless with locks, that it was our error the door was unlocked.

In the end, it was only farm workers who were detained: about twenty of them, taken away to camps to be 'screened'. Half returned within a few days, but the rest, the ones who admitted to having taken the terrorist oaths, or were believed to have secretly drunk the terrorist blood, were kept for 'cleansing', for taking new oaths of loyalty to the government.

Kesi was also picked up by the police. Half-way

through that first day, someone suddenly remembered him, but he was nowhere to be seen. He had waited with Ernest until my father's return and then disappeared. Embarrassed by his failure to perform his duties, and aware that he was unlikely to keep his job, he had resigned, without telling anyone, and had taken his possessions and left. The police found him a couple of days later, but let him go a few days after that.

Only Munyi was never released. I never did find out what the charges against him were, but he pleaded guilty and was hanged. We never saw his family again either. Some time in those first few days they vanished, abandoning their home to the rains, their *shamba* to the bush and the snakes.

My mother was sitting up in bed, brushing her hair, smoothing her curls against her head. She looked flat and colourless. She patted the bed and reached out her hand. When I took it, it felt cold and scrawny, like a chicken's claw.

'I want to go with you, Mum,' I said. 'I want to see Grandpa and Grandma.'

She pulled back her cheeks into a smile and nodded.

'Can I then?' I said.

'What?'

'Can I go with you, to England?'

'No, darling. You have to go to school.'

'But I could go to school in England,' I pleaded, though I wasn't at all sure that this was what I wanted. I was three years old when I left England and I knew my grandparents only from photographs – a grey-haired couple, standing stiffly and peering short-sightedly at the camera – and the presents they sent at Christmas, a penknife that year and a Matchbox double-decker bus the year before.

My mother stroked my cheek gently. 'You have to stay and look after your father,' she said. I opened my mouth to protest but I realized that argument was useless. It was out of her hands now. It was out of all our hands. We were powerless. A stone had been tossed into the water. The ripples spread as they would. There was nothing any of us could do.

After a while, my father came in. 'There's a lot to be done,' he said to the room in general. Then he looked at me. 'Your mother has to pack. You do too. We'll get most of what you need in Nairobi, but lay out what you'd like to take to school and your mother and I can come and look at it later.'

I stood in my bedroom. High in one corner, a gecko lay flat against the ceiling. Before going to the coast I had released all my lizards, and I had not started up a new collection. But this gecko had come to live in my room by its own choice. It clung to the ceiling, its bobbed toes splayed out, its lungs pulsing faintly beneath its mottled pink skin. I moved around the room, running my fingers over my bed, my table, my chair. I picked up a big shell I had brought home from the coast and held it to my ear, listening to the roar of the sea.

On my bed I laid out my book on reptiles, my penknife in its leather pouch, my torch, an arrowhead with dried poison on the tip, six postcards of aeroplanes. I picked up my notebook. Inside was a photograph of my grandparents. I looked at it for a while, and then I went into the living room and took out my parents' photograph album. I found an old picture of my mother and peeled it out and slipped it inside the notebook, which I added to my pile. Finally, I took up Ernest's model Chevrolet and turned it over in my hands. Then I put it away in a drawer. I looked at my possessions on the bed. I was surprised by how little there was.

Later, after lunch, I saw Ernest through the window, cleaning the Chevrolet again. I watched him for a while and then walked out of the front door. The sun had turned the sky white and leached all but the harshest colour from the world. I felt leached too. All I had inside me was a dull ache, a throb of anger. Only Ernest, in his black skin, seemed to have any substance.

'I'm going to proper school,' I told him.

'Good,' he said.

'It's a boarding school. I'll only come back in the holidays. Derek's there already.'

'It is good. You need an education.'

I wanted to provoke him, to hurt him, to punish him, to make him say that he was sorry I was going, that he was going to miss me.

'When I'm finished school,' I said, 'I'm going to university in England. I'm going to be an engineer.'

He looked at me without expression. Then he said, 'That is good,' and returned to washing the car, his hand flat against the cloth, wiping in circles, like the Queen waving on the newsreels they showed in the cinema.

When the afternoon grew cool, I went and sat in the kitchen. Margaret was cooking the roast we would normally have had on a Sunday. I perched on the counter and she gave me a crisp piece of fat. The light was fading, but through the window I could see Ernest out on the steps, reading a book. Something hurt in my gut. There were words I wanted to say to Ernest, but I couldn't get them in the right order. And even if I had been able, I wasn't allowed to go out of the kitchen now. The doors were all locked. Soon Ernest would go inside his room and lock his own door. The terrorists wanted us out, but they would kill him too, if they could, for working for us.

We ate supper early and listened to the evening news. Two days earlier another English family – mother, father and young son – had been killed in their farmhouse. There were calls on the Governor to take more action against the terrorist gangs. The rest of the news of the Trouble was followed by a report on the big flower show in Nairobi. I listened, confused. The newscaster's words seemed to slide into each other, the images to melt together. In one of the films I had seen in town a man had been shot in the belly and the blood had spread on his white shirt like a red rose. I wondered if they gave prizes for that kind of flower.

When the news was over, music came on. No one reached to switch off the radio, and none of us said anything. My mother was wrapped up in her shawl. My father's gun lay on the arm of his chair. I sat back and watched the flames and sparks spitting up the blackened chimney. Fire wasn't like water or air. It wasn't always there. It came out of nothing and returned to nothing. But in between it consumed, it licked at everything around it, and what was flammable disappeared into its blue heart, its red skin, its invisible halo of heat.

Margaret and Gatheru and Ernest and some of the remaining farm workers waved us off the next morning. My mother lay in the back seat, under her shawl, while I had the freedom of the front seat, beside my father. For some reason I remember that journey with peculiar clarity. The hillside glistened as if it was made of gold. I could see every blade of dry grass down the centre of the dirt track, and later, on the tarmac road, every lump of gravel. And when we passed Africans – women with bundles of wood on their backs, men leaning on their spears, honey-sellers holding up their pots – I could see the grain of their irises, the veins on their teeth. A lizard scuttled across the hot road and I had to stop myself from trying to reach out of the window to grab it. I felt I had to fix it all in my memory: as if the whole world was changing, not just our lives; as if I might never come back along this road again; or if I did, it would be altered beyond recognition, the hills sunk into the lakes, the honey-pots crumbled back into dust.

We checked my mother into the hospital and said a muted goodbye. She held me against her and cried softly, but I kept my arms by my side. Then my father and I went to the hotel, where we were sharing a room. We ate supper in the dining room and went to bed early. It was the first time I had slept in the same room as someone else, and I was amazed at the sounds my father made, sighs and grunts and creaks, like a ship at night straining against its anchor.

In the morning we went down to the shops. As we walked a car slowed down and a man looked out at us, his arm on the open window-frame. 'The Governor wants to see you,' he said. 'Go to Government House.' Then he drove away.

The School Shop sold uniforms for all the different schools in the country. I expected my father to scrutinize every item, but instead he handed me over to the shopkeeper and told him to fit me out with all that I needed. He walked away and by the time he came back I had a pile of clothes a foot high: blazer, shorts, shirts, tie, shoes, gym clothes, cricket whites. 'I don't know how to play cricket,' I told the shopkeeper. He looked over his glasses at me. 'Oh, I'm sure you'll learn. Next term it's rugby, but you might have grown by then. Your father can bring you back.'

My father arranged for the clothes to be wrapped up and sent over to the hotel. Out on the streets, it was clear that something was happening. 'Come on,' my father said. 'You might as well see this.' People, white people, were collecting into groups and walking up the road in the same direction. We fell in with a man I recognized from the Hadleys. 'Something's got to be done,' he said to my father.

'Keep up,' my father said to me, swinging his bad leg more quickly. Our route took us away from the centre of town, along a tree-lined avenue. The gates to Government House were open and a large crowd was gathering in front of the great doors. I was soon surrounded by bellies and hips, and by guns – in holsters, hanging from lanyards, poking out of pockets, bags. More people were arriving all the time, pushing the rest of us forward. I was shoved into the bottom of a plump lady in a blue dress and almost stumbled. My father reached down with his big hands and effortlessly lifted me on to his shoulders, from where I had a perfect view. There must have been more than a thousand people already crammed on to the grass and the terrace of the house, and more were coming through the trees behind. In front of us, marshalled by half a dozen European police-men, stood a cordon of African *askaris*, drawn around the house, preventing anyone from reaching the front door. They were sweating in the heat, in their uniforms.

'We want the Governor,' someone shouted. The heads and shoulders below me were packed as close as cattle in a *boma*. 'The Governor!' another voice called, and soon the whole crowd seemed to take up the cry. 'The Governor! The Governor!' I looked around, recog-nizing some of the faces. One of them was Mr Wright. His cheeks were bright red and he was shouting with the rest of them. Then the cry stopped and we all looked up at the house, waiting for the Governor to reply. But the curtains remained closed. 'He'd have to telegraph Whitehall for permission,' someone shouted, and a flurry of horrible laughs and hoots rose up.

In a moment of quiet, a man to our left called out, 'We want our intentions to be clear. I suggest we sing the national anthem.' A few people jeered, but others started singing, and by the second 'God save the Queen' half the crowd had joined in. The song rose up into the hot air. I looked down to see if my father was singing. His mouth was closed. He was not much of a monarchist.

At that point, two European men suddenly appeared from behind the *askaris* and shouted for quiet. 'Please, please,' one of them called. 'It would be better if you all went home. The Governor cannot possibly come out in response to this kind of blackmail. It would set an unfortunate –'

At this a tremendous angry roar went up from the crowd, drowning whatever was said next, and we all surged forward. 'Look, look up there,' a woman screamed, her voice distorted with fury. We all looked up at the façade of Government House and saw a black face staring down at us from a window. 'They've given the house over to the fucking niggers,' the woman continued. 'The bloody bastards!' Beneath me I felt my father shudder, and his hands tightened around my ankles.

Now the screams and cries rose to a crescendo and the crowd flowed forward again. The people at the front were pressed bodily up against the *askaris*, who were struggling to hold the line. At the head of the crowd, I saw a woman's hand reach out and calmly stub her cigarette on an *askari*'s arm. He cried out and drew back. In a moment more cigarettes were lit up, and all down the line I saw women pressing them against black flesh.

Under this pressure it was inevitable that the cordon would break. When it did, the crowd shoved past the *askaris*, and the European policemen, the last line of defence, retreated against the great doors, shouting desperately at the crowd. Now a bearded man only a few feet away from us pulled out his handgun and waved it in the air. His lips were flecked with foam. 'We've got to show the niggers,' someone else cried. The air seemed to blister with invective. 'Kaffirs!' another man yelled, and I saw that it was Mr Wright.

At this moment, a window opened and a blue chair was passed out. People stopped pushing and stared over in curiosity. A tall, rangy man climbed on to the chair and began to shout above the din. Slowly the noise died down and I could hear the wind stirring the leaves of the eucalyptus trees. The man's voice carried clearly and reassuringly. He told everyone to calm down. He offered concessions. I could not understand most of what he said, but I was comforted by his tone, his confidence.

'Is that the Governor?' I whispered to my father.

'Not likely. The Governor's hiding safely inside.'

As the man talked, the anger seemed to evaporate in the hot air and when he called on us all to leave peacefully there were few objections. Slowly people started peeling away from the back and heading quietly out of the grounds. When a space cleared around us, my father put me down and we began to walk too. It was the middle of the day and my head, which had stood out in the sun above the crowd, was aching. I followed my father, two or three paces behind. His left leg dragged slightly and his hips rolled as if we were at sea. Then I remembered there was something I had been wanting to ask him, and I skipped to catch up with him.

'Dad,' I said.

'Yes.'

'Will the baby be born in England?'

'Baby?' He stopped and frowned down at me.

'Yes, the baby. If Mum's in England, will the baby be born there?'

'Baby?' my father said again. 'I thought you knew. The baby's gone. She lost the baby.'

CHAPTER FOUR

'There,' Derek whispered. I wriggled forward on my elbows and lifted my head above the dry grass. The gangster was barely fifty feet away, at the edge of the trees. *Don't shoot until you see the whites of his eyes*, Derek had said. But he was turned away from us. All I could see was the back of his head and his neck as thick and dark as a black python.

'He's mine,' Derek said. He raised his arm and took aim. *Peow*. The silencer muffled the shot. 'Got him.' The gangster rocked from side to side and for a moment I thought he was going to go down. But then he moved on a few paces, lifted the hose pipe, and began to water the next patch of grass on the outfield.

Derek blew on his fingers. 'Good shot, Hadley,' I said. I had learned on my first day not to call him Derek. I could call him Derek at home, but at school it was all surnames. I had also learned that good British boys did not fight the Germans any more, we fought the terrorists, the gangsters, the Kukes, the nigs, the Kafs. In our free time we stalked the gardeners and cleaners and cooks. One boy in my dormitory, Pierce, had even fashioned a sling and took pot-shots with dried beans at passing Africans from the open windows.

Pierce was the opening bat for the cricket team and top boy in our dormitory. Donald was popular because he had a collection of comics. Derek was the youngest, but the most forceful and confident after Pierce. On my second or third night, Derek called me into the lavatory, where I found the other boys from the dormitory waiting for me.

'Take your pyjamas off,' Pierce ordered.

I stared at him blankly.

'We'll take them off for you,' he warned. I stripped and stood there naked while they all urinated on me. Then, still dripping, I had to swear an oath.

'I promise,' Pierce said, for me to repeat, 'to be loyal to the Queen, the Empire and this dormitory.'

'And the Farmers' Association,' Derek added.

'And Denis Compton while we're about it,' Pierce said seriously. 'And I promise to hold as eternal enemies all gangsters.'

'And communists.'

'And never to tell any master about this or anything else.'

'You're lucky we didn't make you kill an Af and drink his blood,' Pierce said dreamily, after I had washed and put my pyjamas back on.

At bedtime, when the lights went out, I lay in the darkness and thought about the farm, my parents, Margaret, Gatheru, Ernest, my bedroom, the gecko on my ceiling. Sometimes, floating at the edge of sleep, I imagined that I was back there myself, that the events of that night had never taken place, that my mother was still at home, the baby still growing inside her belly. But then I would remember, and in that moment of fear it was a relief to breathe in the smell of the other boys, to lie and hear their snuffles and sounds.

Fortunately, the days were too busy for thinking. I wasn't too good at sport, but between them Mrs Wright and my mother and Ernest had schooled me well enough. I was one of the best at maths and good at history, which was taught by the only teacher I liked, an enthusiastic young Scot named McKinnon. I enjoyed the science laboratory too, with its test tubes and Bunsen burners.

It was not hard for me to fit in at school, to blend in. I was a good follower. I watched, and learned quickly. I learned that if you annoyed Pierce he punched you in the stomach; that if you pretended to be friends with Donald he would offer to lend you one of his comics; that Simmons, the piss-a-bed, could be teased with impunity – though even he was to be pitied when Mr Sladdin, the cold-faced maths master, reduced him to tears in front of the class. Mr Sladdin was the worst, because he picked on the weakest. Mr Burton, the Latin teacher, was at his most dangerous when he seemed to be dozing at his desk – a trick, it was said, he had learned while in a Japanese prisoner-of-war camp. Mr Harston had definitely been in the war. 'I spent six years on the lower decks of the Royal Navy for you horrible little animals,' he would bellow at us, his face red with fury. Anybody suspected of misbehaviour was shouted at, kept behind, given lines, caned. But we accepted it all without question. It was the masters' job to catch us out, to humiliate us.

My parents wrote periodically – brief, distant letters about the farm and Worcester, sun and snow, that I read once and then put away. What mattered now was school life: tests, teachers, friends, enemies, food. One night, though, early on, I was quizzed about the incident at our farm.

'How many were there?' Pierce asked me, after the lights went out.

'How many what?'

'How many gangsters that attacked your house? Twenty? Thirty? Forty?'

'Twenty,' I said, erring on the side of caution.

'What weapons did they have?'

'A *panga*.'

'A *panga*?'

'*Pangas* and *simis* – and bows and arrows.'

'What about guns?'

'One had a gun.'

'My father came back to the house with his father,' Derek interrupted, and I was thankful that Derek had been at school when it happened and did not know the truth.

'Why didn't they kill you?' Pierce asked.

'My mother shot them,' I said.

'What, all of them?'

'No, just enough to send them packing.'

This seemed to satisfy Pierce and the others. I imagine most of them guessed I was exaggerating, but they didn't seem to mind. It was a good story. After that I don't think I once talked about the farm. As the weeks passed I thought about it less and less, and when the end of term arrived it caught me by surprise. When I had first come to school I had concentrated on how to survive the first day, the first week. If I had thought about the distant end of term, it was with the vague assumption that by the time it arrived my mother would be back, the Trouble would be over, I might even be returning to Mrs Wright's. But now the term was almost finished and my father's last letter had mentioned no such happenings. When the parents arrived to collect, only Ernest was with my father.

We were giving Derek a lift home and he and I sat in the back, while Ernest drove and my father rode shotgun, his revolver on his lap.

'Is Ernest a Kikuyu?' Derek whispered to me.

'Half.'

'That's enough,' he replied confidently.

Enough for what? I didn't know. The memory of Ernest in the corridor came into my head – his hand thrusting violently at me, his harsh voice as he spoke to Munyi.

When the police had questioned me that next day, I had tried to tell them my theory – that it was all a mistake, that Munyi had only come to get medicine from my mother. The sergeant had not been interested, but later on, lying awake in those first nights at school, I had repeated the story to myself, and in doing so I had come to the conclusion that it was all Ernest's fault. If Ernest hadn't come into the house Munyi would have had a chance to tell my mother about his sickness and everything would have been all right. It was Ernest who had panicked Munyi, who had frightened my mother. It was Ernest's fault that Munyi and the other workers had been taken away, that my mother was in England, that the baby was dead.

I sat back against the seat of the car and stared at Ernest's sinewy neck in front of me as he drove, and tried to feel angry.

We dropped Derek off and drove past the *dukas* and along the familiar track home. The house was empty without my mother, and the farm was depressingly quiet. Although my father had hired two new guards, a dozen of the workers were still in detention, and we had not taken on anyone else in their place. The rains were late, and a blanket of heat and dust lay over the farm. My father was working harder than ever, but he seemed to take no satisfaction from his labour. Most of the grass had been eaten or burned away and the brown earth was cracking beneath the brutal sun. The cattle were doing well enough; there was water in the lake and feed in the stores. But the men seemed dried out, their skin loose and flaking, pale pink dust on their faces and in their hair.

There had been no more trouble on the farm, but I was strictly forbidden to walk about on my own. When I wasn't accompanying my father on his rounds, I sat in the cool corner of the kitchen, away from the oven. Margaret's cooking still tasted delicious when I picked at it in the kitchen, but the silent suppers with my father seemed to drain the flavour from the food. When an invitation arrived to visit Derek, I felt only relief.

Easter Friday was just a couple of days away and, in contrast to the emptiness I had left behind at home, the Hadleys' house was already half full of visitors – friends from England, suitors for Derek's sisters, even a journalist writing about the Emergency – with the prospect of more arriving for the weekend. Once, in a moment of quiet, my mind turned to my father, spending Easter alone, and for that moment I felt sorry for him. But then Derek pulled at my shirt and I was tugged away to brighter thoughts.

Derek and I were not allowed to stray outside the grounds, but his house and gardens were so much bigger than mine that we did not feel boxed in. We gossiped about school, played matador with the Hadleys' pet duiker, and spied on everyone else. That week there was also the excitement of laying eyes on a real terrorist – the only one I was to see throughout the Trouble. It was the second night of my visit and Mr Hadley had gone out with one of the newly formed settlers' commandos. Derek and I were woken by the sounds of several vehicles rolling into the drive, followed by hushed but excited voices. We could not see on to the drive from Derek's room, so we put on our dressing gowns and crept down the stairs. The front door was open and the outdoor lights were on. Three or four pick-ups and jeeps were pulled up on the drive, and a couple of young men were leaning against one, sipping at mugs of steaming coffee.

'I popped one at least,' one of them said, his eyes glinting, his pale blond hair glowing in the lights.

'I hit one too, heard him squeal, but then I lost him.'

'You should have seen my one's face. He can't have been more than ten feet away when he saw me.'

'How many have you got now?'

'Three.'

'Not bad.'

'I would have had the bastard in the pick-up too,' the

blond man said, nodding over his head. 'Only I shouted halt and he halted. Can you believe that?'

He produced a packet of cigarettes and they both lit up. The tips burned like fireflies. 'Should we check on him?' the darker of the two said, nodding over his shoulder.

'No, he's trussed up like a chicken.'

'Right.'

'Did you hear about Tony?'

'Yeah, the Kuke was just about to take off his head with a *simi* when John Hadley intervened.'

'Close thing.'

'Too close.'

Derek nudged me, his eyes alight with pride. 'Come on,' he whispered.

'What?'

'Let's go and look.'

I followed him along the wall and then around the blind side of the nearest jeep, towards the pick-up the men had indicated. They hadn't noticed us. They were talking again now, and we crept across a stretch of open ground, hearts beating, as if reliving the events they were describing. When we arrived at the pick-up, Derek pulled himself up on to the back bumper and I followed him, clambering up, my heart beating so loudly now I was sure that every gang in Africa would hear me, not just the monstrous gangster I was about to see.

I kept my eyes closed, and then slowly opened them. I had heard about the terrorists a thousand times, but I had never until that moment properly considered who they were, what they were – and I can still remember my disappointment that the figure lying beneath us did not have scales, or claws, or was not breathing fire. He was small and skinny and human, and lay there unmoving. He was wrapped around and around with rope, his arms pinned to his side, his legs bound together, his mouth gagged. Only his hair was wild and frightening, long and matted, with mud and leaves tangled up in it. His head was upside-down, but when my eyes adjusted to the angle, I saw how young he was – a boy, only a few years older than us, no more than fifteen or sixteen. Instinctively, without realizing what I was doing, I smiled at him, and through his own fear or hatred or whatever was lurking inside his head, his eyes smiled back at me, the both of us acknowledging, for that moment, despite all else that lay between us, some community of boyhood. And then we both recognized what we were doing, what loyalties we were betraying, and in unison I frowned furiously down at him and he turned away from me. He began to writhe against the ropes, twisting and groaning, until he was exhausted, and he lay still again, his breath rattling in his nose and thick froth bubbling up from one nostril.

'Derek! What on earth –' It was Mr Hadley, striding towards us. We leaped down guiltily from the bumper. 'What do you two think you are doing?'

'He's tied up, Dad,' Derek protested.

'I don't care if he's chained to the floor. Back to bed, right away.' He stood, with his legs apart, and clipped us both on the head as we passed.

On the Saturday night the guests gathered for a formal dinner. Derek and I were given supper early and were supposed to be up in our bedroom, out of the way, but when everyone was in the dining room, we crept out again and sat in the shadows half-way down the stairs, peeking through the partly open door and listening to the talk. The women were wearing long dresses and the men dinner jackets. Glasses of wine sparkled in the candlelight and silver surrounded every place. And in front of most of the diners lay squat L-shaped chunks of gun metal, adding their own peculiar dull lustre to the occasion.

From where I sat, I could see Rose, Derek's elder sister, laughing and flirting with the blond-haired young man from the previous night. She leaned towards him and showed him her glorious front teeth, and he looked far less confident than he had been out in the darkness, his gun still hot from shooting. Everyone was talking at once and, with the sounds of drinking and eating, only the odd phrase or snatch of talk drifted out to us. But then half the conversations seemed to run dry at the same moment, and one man's voice, though not raised, carried clearly to where Derek and I crouched.

'Ninety, probably more. Some of them must have crept away into the bush to die.' I couldn't see who was speaking, but I recognized the voice as belonging to Anne's suitor, a young man in the army or police.

'You were at Lari?' This was the journalist, breaking in.

'I was there the day after.'

'It must have been horrible,' a woman's voice added.

'Not very pleasant,' Anne's suitor said with a dry laugh.

'All those poor women and children.'

'Yes,' he said quietly. 'Everywhere you –'

'I really don't think this is the place,' another woman interrupted.

'– you looked,' he continued, and a certain quality in his voice quietened the whole room. 'They didn't spare anyone. Not even babies. It was – a kind of madness.'

'I don't see what all the fuss is about,' a man I could see through the doorway said haughtily. He had a long face and a streak of grey in his black hair and looked like a zebra. 'Kukes killing Kukes.'

'Henry!'

'No, let them is what I say. Saves us the trouble. It's none of our business what they do to each other.'

'It's our business what happens in our country.' I recognized this voice, Mr Hadley. 'As long as we are in charge of this land, it's our duty to keep the peace.'

'We,' another man snorted. 'We are not in charge. The bloody Governor's in charge. Whitehall.'

'Yes,' Mr Hadley said softly. 'But we're working on that.'

'It's the cattle I object to,' came a new voice, slightly slurred with drink. 'My best milker. Didn't even kill the poor girl. Cut out her eyes and left her.'

'The eyes? What for?'

'Don't ask.'

'Ugh. A touch more wine please.'

The talk broke up again into smaller eddies, and Derek and I retreated to his room. He had filched a box of chocolates and one of his father's cigars, and we sat up, eating ourselves sick and trying to draw smoke through the roughly cut end of the cigar. We were still awake when we heard the bay windows open below us and the voices of the men filter out into the garden.

'Watch this,' Derek said, and I joined him by the window. The men lined up against the stone wall, facing away from us. For a moment I thought it was something to do with the Trouble, some military man-oeuvre. But then I heard a hissing, and saw the steam rising up from the stonework.

'To Africa,' someone said, and the rest repeated the toast, the words floating out into the night.

'Good, eh?' Derek said. 'Dad says Africa's the best place in the whole world. The communists won't chase us away.'

I stared out into the darkness. The terrorists were out there somewhere, watching, waiting, ready to swoop down on a farm or an unsuspecting village. I knew the horrible things they did. But at that moment I couldn't help feeling sorry for them. They didn't know what they were up against. Oaths and *pangas* and forest hideouts were nothing beside the insouciance I had just wit-nessed. The best the gangsters could hope for, like Mag-witch in *Great Expectations*, was a good pork pie before the end.

That year Edmund Hillary and Sherpa Tensing reached the summit of Mount Everest, Elizabeth climbed the steps of Westminster Abbey to be crowned, and Im-perial Airways' new de Havilland Comets reduced the flying time between London and Nairobi to eighteen hours and forty minutes – but my mother kept her feet firmly on the streets of Worcester, and it was not until the following February, during my second Lent term at school, that she finally wrote to say she was coming home.

I read the letter several times, to make sure, and then put it in my pocket.

'My mother's coming back,' I told Derek, listening to the sound of the words.

'Is her snakebite better?'

'Yes,' I said. 'She's fine now.'

Inside I wasn't so confident. For a start, her letters had been oddly distant and disconnected – as if they had been written from somewhere even further away than England. And then, when I closed my eyes to picture her, I found, to my dismay, that I could not remember what she looked like. All I could see was the face from the photograph I had brought with me – an eighteen-year-old version of my mother, smiling coyly at the camera, as strange to me as if she was someone else entirely. That evening, I went into the bathroom and looked in the mirror. *You've got your mother's eyes*, someone had once told me. I held my hand over my mouth and nose and peered at the reflection, but only my own eyes looked back, unblinking, mocking me.

When the last day of term arrived, we all got up early. I put on my blazer and tied my tie four times before the knot was right. But I still felt scruffy, itchy, uncomfortable, as if my clothes were the wrong ones, as if I had put on someone else's skin. I stood by the window and watched as the cars turned through the gate. When the Chevrolet finally appeared, I ran down the stairs and out of the big front door. My father was standing by the car and I looked through the windscreen at the figure sitting inside. It was only Ernest, again.

'Where's Mum?'

'At home,' my father said. 'She's still a little tired from the journey.'

'When did she get home?'

'A week ago.'

I looked out of the open window. It had barely rained a drop in a year and a half and the land was brown and dry and cracked in every direction. Some time later we drove over the rise and rattled slowly down towards the house. I peered out through the dust, and as we pulled up under the barren flame tree, the front door opened and my mother came out to meet me.

'You've grown,' she said, stroking my cheek dreamily. I frowned up at her, wanting her to know that she couldn't just go away and come back whenever she liked, but she didn't seem to notice. She reached down and brushed her lips against my forehead, and the smell of some new English perfume mingled with the scent of her own body and the gritty odour of the dust like someone else's version of the past, familiar and strange all at once.

'Come on,' my father said. 'Let's go into the shade. You don't want to risk getting another migraine.'

She didn't argue. Her perfume, and her fashionable clothes, a yellow dress and shiny shoes, couldn't hide her frailness. There were new lines on her neck and around her mouth, and when I touched her, I felt the bones beneath her skin.

She had about her, I realized over the next day or two, the same air of detachment I had picked up from her letters. The first time we went out into the garden together and looked at the dusty lawn and the dry flower-beds, only the hardiest plants sprouting spiky blossoms, she blinked in bewilderment, as if she couldn't quite understand how she had come back to this.

Through her eyes, I also saw how much the farm had suffered in her absence, how much of our old life had crumbled with the baked hillside. As well as the lake drying out and the crops failing, Margaret had left us. Her son – a son I had not even known existed until he was dead – had been killed in the Trouble and she had returned to the reserves to help look after his family and land. The workforce was also depleted. Some of the detainees had been released and had come back to the farm, but other squatters had left, drifting off from fear or disaffection to the reserves and forests. Those who remained had been moved into huts in a high stockade below the farm buildings. Here they could be both watched over and watched – for, as Mr Hadley cheerfully put it, 'You never know whether your *watu* are more likely to kill you or be killed for working for you.' When, two or three days after I returned, my mother held her first afternoon clinic, the Africans who gathered on the lawn seemed more listless than sick. The drought and the Trouble and the crowded stockade had worn away at them, and several times I had to rouse both my mother and her patient from simply sitting and staring at the cloudless sky. The only thing that really brought my mother to life was talking about the Coronation, which she had watched on television. 'It was the most wonderful sight in the world,' she whispered whenever the subject was raised. 'The Queen was more beautiful than Rita Hayworth.'

The days passed without a hint of cloud, and just as it seemed that the rains were going to fail again, a wind suddenly picked up, and by the evening I was tasting the cool, damp, slightly rank flavour of water in the air. It didn't rain that night, or the next day, though the sky filled with billowing bruisers of clouds, blue and black and purple. But the second night the storm broke and I lay in bed listening to the water beating down and watching the room light up every time the lightning cracked.

'Time to get up.' I opened my eyes and saw my father standing over the bed. 'Up, up.' It was barely morning, but the storm had passed and there was no time to be lost. The fields had to be ploughed and sown, and every hand was needed, even me. I pulled on my clothes and followed my father out on to the porch, where he was drinking a steaming cup of tea and surveying the land glistening anew in the grey dawn light.

All that week, while my father drove the tractor back and forth across the hillside, turning over the clods of earth, I worked alongside the Africans, planting, fertilizing, fetching, digging. Under the sun, between the bursts of rain, my skin burned darker, and my arms and legs thickened and grew stronger with the physical labour. The rain seemed to have infused my veins with new life. And all around me it was the same. The soft furrows in the earth reaffirmed the meaning of the farm, the pattern of life. My mother's flowerbeds were exploding with colour, and some of her old strength had returned too. The rain had washed away the dust, and the faces of the Africans, of all of us, gleamed like the face of the world, dripping with moisture and promise.

One evening, after dark, my father strode into the living room, soil in his hair and in the grain of his skin and the roots of his nails. 'This morning I drove the tractor into the sun as it rose over the hill and this evening I was still driving when it sank beneath the end of the field,' he said. They were the most poetic words we had ever heard him say, and for a moment my mother's face brightened as if he had mentioned the Coronation, and the dullness lifted from her eyes. After she had tucked me into bed I waited for the sound of music on the gramophone, and when it came I tiptoed down the corridor and looked through the crack in the door. My father was holding my mother in his arms and they were dancing slowly around the floor. He had his big hand on her waist, and he moved it down on to her bottom and pressed his mouth against her delicate lips.

'Philip, stop.'

She turned her face from his, and he pulled back.

'I don't –' she began. 'I can't, not yet.'

He whispered something to her I could not hear, and then he pulled her close again and his arms enclosed her. I stole quietly back to the warmth of my bed.

In those first days of the rains, Ernest was working in the fields as well, and I saw more of him then than I had done in the year since I had gone away to school. The sinews tautened on his neck and wrists as he worked, and sweat gathered in tiny droplets on his nose, like jewels on black silk.

'*Habari ya* school?' he said one afternoon, while we were standing side by side.

'All right.'

'You must know so much now.'

I shrugged and bent down towards the soil again. But

when I glanced at him out of the corner of my eye and saw how wholeheartedly he worked, how he gave himself over to his honest labour, I suddenly wanted to talk to him again.

'We've got science labs,' I said. 'We dissected a frog. If you pull the tendon you can make its leg bend, even though it's dead. I'm not very good at cricket.'

'Ee.' He nodded, and smiled, and I felt the warmth of his smile again, its encouragement.

'Pierce is the best bat. He's the biggest in our dormitory. He shone his magnifying glass in Mr Sladdin's eye and got caned by the headmaster. Mr Sladdin's the maths teacher.'

There was not much talk while we worked. Sometimes a comment was made, or a joke that spread across the field, but apart from the occasional song, we toiled most of the time to the sounds of our own labour, the squelch of the earth, the rasp of our breathing, the rattling of the tractor. But when we broke for tea, or stood waiting for the tractor to move on, Ernest and I began to talk, to catch up, to pay attention to each other. I told him about school, and he began to talk again of his life, his dreams. And as we talked, as we went over old ground and new thoughts, something began to itch inside my head, half a memory of half an idea somewhere in my skull. One day Ernest stopped and looked down the hillside, green and wet, mist clinging to the slopes beneath us.

'Today it is like his island.'

I looked at the hillside suspiciously.

'When it was wet like this Father always talked about his island,' he added.

I said nothing, but my head was itching again, and that afternoon, when I glanced down at a magazine, a Coronation souvenir my mother had brought home with her, the itch suddenly become a whole idea. QUEEN OF GREAT BRITAIN AND NORTHERN IRE-LAND. I stared at the words. I had seen them before, but now I saw them in a different way. I looked at the clock. It was five minutes to six. I ran into the kitchen and pushed through the door. Ernest's door was closed, but I banged on it.

He opened it dressed only in his trousers.

'Ernest,' I cried, 'what island was your father from?'

He looked down at me in surprise. 'I'll put my shirt on,' he said, turning away.

'No!' The urgency in my own voice startled me, but I knew that any moment I would be called in and the doors locked. 'How do you spell it?' I demanded.

'Spell?'

'How do you spell his island?'

A fly buzzed between us and he brushed it away. Then, slowly he said, 'I-R-E-L-A-N-D.'

'Ireland? Like Northern Ireland?'

'*Ndio*. In actual fact he was from Southern Ireland, but he said it was all the same place. He said one day it would be united again.'

'Then he was Irish?' I knew about the Irish, I had heard about them in history lessons. There was even an Irish farmer in the highlands, a man with a face like a weasel.

'Yes.'

'But how could he be your father?' The more I understood, the more confused I became.

'He wasn't my real father,' he said softly. 'I've told you I'm half Kikuyu. My father was a Kikuyu. This one was Father. That is what we called him. Wait, I can show you.'

He disappeared inside and came back with a photograph, a fuzzy, crumpled black and white shot. In it I saw a younger Ernest, and beside him an old white man, fat and jolly, with a white beard, like Father Christmas. For a bewildering moment I thought that this was what Ernest was trying to tell me, that his father was Father Christmas.

'Father,' Ernest said. 'Father Patrick. He was a priest, a Catholic priest. He had a church school in Nyeri. He took me in when I was a boy, only a little bit older than you. He had an old Ford, you've heard me tell you many times.'

Ernest never knew his real father, and could not remember his mother. She was a Luo from the lands that bordered the great lake, and he was a Kikuyu. All he knew of his father was that he had visited his mother's area several times and was a truck driver – and that his mother had fallen in love with him and become pregnant. She was very young, perhaps only thirteen or fourteen, and her parents were angry, for she was promised to another man. And by the time her pregnancy was discovered, Ernest's father had disappeared, never to return. Ernest's mother carried her son until she gave birth and then died – from a broken heart, Ernest said, though I imagine that the bacteria that killed so many Africans in those days must have played a part too.

Ernest was brought up by his grandparents. His grandfather was a village chief and a wealthy man, with land and cows, and Ernest was fortunate to have the opportunity to attend the only school in the area. He did well at school, outstripping all the other children (his father's thrusting Kikuyu blood perhaps) and by the age of eleven or twelve there was no more his teacher could teach him.

By then Ernest was already fascinated with anything mechanical. In those days, the passing of a car or truck was enough of an event for the adults to join the children at the trackside, waving and staring at the vehicle. But Ernest was the most enchanted by these brief visits from the world beyond. After all the others had returned to work or rest, Ernest would still be standing on the road, watching the dust settle and examining the tyre tracks. In the holidays he several times walked barefoot the fifteen miles down to the lake in the hope of catching sight of a big boat steaming through the water, and once he walked for three days to the railway line to see the train he had only heard and read about.

It was after this journey that Ernest decided he would go in search of his father, the truck driver, the traveller from the wondrous mechanical world beyond. One night, when everyone else was asleep, he collected his few possessions – two or three books and a spare shirt – and left a note that his grandparents would not themselves have been able to read, and stole out of the hut. It was 1943 and all across the world men were at war. But Ernest knew little of this. He was concerned only with his own campaign, to find his father, to become a truck driver like him.

He walked until he came to the main road. He knew

the train went all the way to the city, in the heart of Kikuyuland, but he had no money to pay for a ticket, and anyway he hoped that by riding in trucks he might hear word of his father. The drivers were intrigued by his quest – many of them knew or suspected that they had fathered children themselves along their routes – and they carried Ernest without asking for money. But none of them could help with Ernest's father. Ernest did not even know the man's name: if his grandparents had known it themselves, they had refused to reveal it. All he could tell them was the name of his own village, the village his father must have driven through to meet his mother, but there was no regular truck route that passed that way.

When he reached Nairobi, Ernest was dazzled and bemused. On his journey he had grown used to cars and trucks and roads and new people. But here was modern life in such profusion that he did not know where to turn. The people were too busy to listen to his questions, impatient with his few halting words of Swahili. He was not offered hospitality, as strangers would have been in his own village, and he had no money and did not want to steal. By his second day he was starving. When another boy, an urchin half his age, tried to rob him of his small bundle, Ernest turned his back on the city and walked until he came to a petrol station, where he found a ride on a truck heading north to the Kikuyu reserves. In the hills life was slower and Ernest had time to ask about his father. The people were more generous, and gave him food and shelter. But no one could help with his quest, and it was at the very moment that Ernest was beginning to accept that he would never find his father – perhaps, in the strange ways of the world, partly because he was beginning to accept this – that he stumbled across the next best thing. For just as Ernest needed a father, Father Patrick was in his own way looking for a son.

Father Patrick had devoted his life to God, but around his fiftieth birthday, shortly before Ernest arrived, he had suffered a loss of faith. He had never been the most holy of men. He enjoyed whisky and food and tinkering beneath the bonnet of his old Ford as much as any heathen, and while his new doubts made no difference to the satisfaction he took from helping people less fortunate than himself, he felt oddly empty. God had filled a gap in his life. The part of him that needed to love had loved God. And now that he doubted God, he found himself in need of an earthly substitute.

The afternoon that Ernest arrived, Father Patrick was taking apart the engine of his Ford. Ernest sat and watched him, much as I, years later, had sat and watched Ernest working on the Chevrolet. By that evening, Ernest had begun to take a place in Father Patrick's heart. Father Patrick gave Ernest a room in the servants' quarters, and a few months later he took him into the house, and though he never officially adopted Ernest, he treated him like a son. He shared his thoughts and dreams with him, and bought him clothes and books, and put him through school. It was Father Patrick who first told Ernest that he must go to university to become an engineer.

Father Patrick was not yet sixty when he suffered his heart attack. In the few hours before he died, he gave Ernest his treasured tool kit and his collection of

National Geographic magazines, and wrote a letter to his church in Ireland outlining his plans for Ernest. But three months later, when Father Patrick's replacement arrived from Ireland, the new priest was horrified to find Ernest living in the house. This priest was not a bad man but he seemed to know nothing about any plans to send Ernest to university. And he could not countenance Ernest living on in the house. Perhaps he came to mistaken conclusions about the nature of the love between Ernest and Father Patrick. He did what he could, writing the letter of recommendation which helped Ernest secure the job with Mr Cartwright, the farmer from whom my father had purchased the Chevrolet.

Ernest was nineteen then, the same intelligent, eager young man who had been heading for university to study engineering. But he had lost his sponsor, he had lost the white man who could help him. His brain and skills and character were no longer the qualities by which the world would judge him. Without Father Patrick to write letters and organize funds, Ernest was simply another African.

He worked for Mr Cartwright for a year. Then Mr Cartwright decided to return to Europe. He sold his Chevrolet to my father and threw Ernest in as well – an afterthought, a free extra, like a jack or a spare tyre.

Ernest told me this over the days that followed, during breaks from work, at the ends of afternoons, in bits and pieces, in chapters. I say chapters because though I believe that most of what he said was true – all of it essentially – it had the shape and consistency of a story.

Once he began talking he barely hesitated until we were interrupted, and when he had occasion to go over a part again, he repeated himself almost word for word. At the time, in my contrition for ever having doubted him, I took this as evidence of the absolute truth of what he said. But now it seems to me that he must have for years been shaping the story in his head, refining it, making his past fit for the future, the destiny that he still believed, in his own dreamy way, despite the false turns he had taken, was waiting for him.

In fact, as I now learned, Ernest's chances of attaining this destiny had improved. After the police had taken Munyi away, my father had, in gratitude for Ernest's prompt action, promised that when the Emergency was over, he would do all he could to help Ernest get to university. Discovering this helped me to forgive my father for misleading me about Ernest – or at least gave me an excuse not to think too much about it. For while I did not believe that my father had deliberately set me against Ernest, the alternative, that my father could have been so wrong about something, was equally disturbing to countenance. So I didn't countenance it. I simply allowed myself to accept that two contrary versions of the world could exist side by side, just as I talked of niggers and Kaffirs at school and then came home to my friends Gatheru and Ernest in the holidays. It was easy. I was getting good at duplicity. I was growing up.

The rains that revived the farm had not washed away the Trouble. If anything, the Emergency had intensified, as the gangsters and soldiers battled to outwit each other on the farms and in the forests. The vast majority of the dead and mutilated were Africans, though that holiday I remember listening to the radio report the killing of a four-year-old European boy snatched from his garden while riding his tricycle. But even that upset me only for a day or two. Life went on. We simply adapted to its changes, and each *panga* slash served merely to thicken the scar tissue that all of us had grown.

With Gatheru busy in the kitchen and the house, Ernest had taken over the shopping duties and twice a week he drove the Chevrolet down to the *dukas*. Once during those holidays, we all accompanied him. My mother wanted to choose something from the shops herself, and my father came along to provide protection. The *dukas*, which only a year earlier had been just a couple of shops, an African *hoteli* and a petrol station, had expanded with the Trouble into a small town. Africans from all over the region had moved here for safety, and hundreds of huts and shacks, made from scraps of wood, bits of rusty corrugated iron, sheets of plastic and the round bottoms of oil barrels, had sprung up along the road and back into the bush behind. When we drove through the crowded main street, dogs slouched out of our way, children ran along behind us and old men sitting in the shade followed us with their eyes.

My father and I waited by the car while my mother chose some material in a shop and Ernest went from stall to stall, prodding the food, picking it up, bargaining over the price. To my surprise, everyone seemed to know him, and they greeted him by name and shook his hand. One old woman even said something suggestive to him, and all the men around laughed and pushed him forward, slapping him on his back. For the first time I realized that Ernest had an existence beyond what I knew of him – that he too straddled more than one world, just as I did.

In the middle of the Easter holidays, a new addition to the household arrived. Mary was almost young enough to be Margaret's granddaughter, and could not cook or iron or even clean in the right way, until Gatheru taught her. But she had worked for an English family, and could speak English, and, most importantly, she was not a Kikuyu. She was a Luo, from the west, like half of Ernest.

She was shy, but pretty, and I soon realized that Ernest liked her. During the day, when he had a moment, he would appear outside the kitchen, hoping for a sight of her, and sometimes in the late afternoons, when I stole out through the kitchen to catch him before the doors were locked, I would find him talking to her. Then, through a chink in her shyness, I would see something of the look I often saw on Derek's sisters' faces, and Ernest would gulp and grin like those sisters' suitors, like a dog eager for scraps.

'Are you going to marry Mary?' I asked Ernest one afternoon, when she was cleaning inside.

'Marry?' he spluttered.

'Well, are you?' I said, determined to find out.

'Where did you get this idea?'

'I saw you.'

He thought for a moment, perhaps wondering what I had seen, and then he said, 'We've only just met.'

'My father only spent one afternoon on the Malvern Hills with my mother and they had to get married.'

'Ee!' He looked at me in amazement, and finally laughed.

I frowned at him. I wanted to be taken seriously, but he wasn't to be drawn on the subject.

On any other matter, however, he was more than willing to talk. With the fields under crop, and the farm work slackening off, there was more time, and I spent as much as I could of the remaining days of the holidays with him, down at the farm buildings, or by the house, working on the vehicles. He talked and talked, telling me more about engineering, about Sir Malcolm Campbell's *Blue Bird*, the George Washington Bridge, the passenger aircraft that were shrinking the word, and I listened eagerly, no longer doubting a word he said. At times his words even induced in me a kind of drunkenness and I would melt contentedly into his dreams, his imagination, happy to abandon the thrummings of my own thoughts. I have, I suppose, a tendency to be easily led, and I might count myself lucky that my childhood left me with a stomach that cannot handle drink, for otherwise, in my moments of weakness, of loneliness, without some person to inspire me, I might easily have succumbed to the authority and easy oblivions of alcohol.

The last night of the holidays, as I went to close my curtains, I saw the moon glowing behind the purple clouds, and I remembered again what Ernest had said on the beach.

'Will people really go to the moon?' I asked him the next morning.

'They will,' he said, his head under the hood of the Chevrolet. He fiddled about for a while and then came out, wiping his hands on a rag. 'In fact, the moon could be the answer.'

'What answer?'

'To all these land problems,' he said, as if his meaning was obvious. 'The moon is a whole world. If the land is good, maybe some of the British will go there to farm.'

'Farm the moon?'

'*Ndio*. It could be. They can go to the moon and there will be room in the highlands for the Africans again. Perhaps even some Africans can get land on the moon too.'

He laughed at the brilliance of his idea.

'You know,' he said, 'when my grandfather first saw a British man many years ago, he thought he was from the moon, his face was so white.'

At school, the talk was all about Mr Burton, the Latin teacher, who was taken ill after the first week and did not appear again that term. A rumour started up that he had gone mad, that his years in a Japanese prisoner-of-war camp, eating only rice, had finally done for him, and as the weeks passed other evidence emerged to suggest the madness had been there all along. Several boys admitted that he had put his hands down their trousers. This on its own was not particularly damning, as the cricket master put his hand down all our whites to check that we weren't wearing underpants. But another boy then spoke of going back to Mr Burton's room and being asked to drop a medicine ball on to Mr Burton's bare stomach. After that the stories grew wilder and wilder: Mr Burton had run naked through the grounds one night, Mr Burton was a spy, Mr Burton was not really ill – he had been kidnapped by the terrorists and buried alive.

I played my part in these discussions, and in everything else, but that term I found it hard to engage properly with school life. I felt half a step behind the other boys, companion to their shadows. The walls around the grounds, which had previously seemed to contain a whole world, now closed in around me claustrophobically. Sometimes I went to the gate and stared down the road. Every night I fell asleep thinking about the farm, my mother, Ernest, and when morning came I was invariably disappointed to find myself still at school.

For the first time, I counted down the weeks, and when the last few days arrived, I became fidgety and jittery, like Simmons and the other boys who did not fit in.

My father came as always to fetch me in the Chevrolet, but this time he was on his own.

'Mum's at home?' I said, seeking reassurance.

'Yes.'

'Where's Ernest?'

'Come on,' he said. 'We'd better get going.'

The cars left the grounds in a long queue, and it was only after several miles, when the roads branched, that everyone headed in different directions and the road cleared ahead of us.

'I'm afraid we've lost Ernest,' my father said.

'Lost?' When I had collected lizards I sometimes lost them. They crawled through cracks, hid beneath the bed. But Ernest was too big to lose.

'It was only last week. The police took him away.'

'They took Ernest?'

'Yes, seems he'd got involved with the terrorists.' I looked up at my father, half expecting him to tell me it was all a joke, but he glanced down at me sympathetically. 'I found it hard to believe myself,' he continued. 'But the police had no doubts. There was nothing I could do. Apparently he was foolish enough to make a speech in front of half a dozen police informers down at the *dukas*. Talked about the British leaving, Africans taking over the highlands. Some of it was in code, apparently.'

'Code?' I whispered.

'Yes. Something about the British going off to farm the moon, whatever that was supposed to mean.'

My mouth was suddenly dry.

'I wouldn't have thought it of a good fellow like Ernest,' my father continued, shaking his head sadly. 'Always a hard worker. But that's what this Trouble has achieved.'

CHAPTER FIVE

One Saturday morning, a year or so after Ernest's arrest, Mr Hadley arrived at our farm in his new silver sports car. He had brought another man, Captain Alec Smith, to meet my father, and when they shook hands I saw veins like fat blue worms throbbing beneath the skin above Captain Smith's knuckles. I stayed outside for a while, admiring the car, a four-cylinder convertible Sunbeam Talbot Mr Hadley had just shipped over from England, and then went back into the house. My father had taken the guests out on to the veranda, and I tiptoed into the living room and settled on to the sofa.

'Not to mention the Capricorn Society,' Mr Hadley said, his words drifting in through the open doors. 'It's just a question of looking after our own future. Alec here –'

'I'm not a politician,' Captain Smith took over, his voice more earthy than Mr Hadley's, but just as persuasive and sure of itself. 'I'm a farmer like you, like John. But I'm damned if I'm going to let the Lennox-Boyds of this world decide our future. What does he care about Africa? It's us who have sweated to make something of these hills, who have almost lost our wives to malaria, who have raised our children under this hot sun. To Lennox-Boyd, Africa is a question of policy, to us it's our home, our children's future.'

I knew who Lennox-Boyd was, the Colonial Secretary. I had heard him on the radio: the Emergency, gathering families around their radio sets every night, had made political experts of all of us. Lennox-Boyd had come out from London the previous year and I remembered his dry English voice offering reassurances on the news.

'India,' Captain Smith was saying.

'The Gold Coast now,' Mr Hadley added. I knew about the Gold Coast too, and its African prime minister, Dr Nkrumah.

I waited for my father to speak, curious what he would say, but it was the other men who continued, their alternating voices reminding me of a comic double act we sometimes listened to on the radio.

'The *watu* don't want this so-called multiracialism, not your average Kuke.'

'It's the communists.'

'The Hindis.'

'You just have to look at the evidence.'

'It's simple. As long as we remain united, we can carry on building the kind of future we want.'

'Oh, there you are.'

I looked up. My mother was standing in the doorway. She walked slowly across the room and closed the French doors, shutting out the voices from the veranda. 'I need your help,' she said. 'In the garden.' We walked around the house, so as not to disturb the men, and made our way down to where the scarlet cannas and golden lilies stared unblinkingly at the sun.

While I helped my mother, my mind turned to Ernest. The Sunbeam Talbot had reminded me of him, and I realized, with a vague sense of disloyalty, that I had not thought about him for weeks. Since his arrest, his name had barely been mentioned. In the car on the way home from school, when my father had told me how the police had come and taken Ernest away, I had wanted to explain to my father what Ernest meant about the moon, to make my father go straight to the police station and get him released. But somehow I had been unable. I was paralysed. When I tried to speak, I was stopped by the memory of the policemen's faces the day Munyi was taken away, polite but unreachable, unbelieving.

At some point in the following months I had heard that Ernest had been tried and sentenced to prison, but that was all. I had wondered at first whether he would write, whether I should write to him, but then I decided that he probably wasn't allowed to send or receive letters, and I left it at that. It was easier to let go of the past than to hold on to it, and I tried to think only of the day ahead, the morning, the afternoon, the next dawn unfurling at the horizon.

In this perhaps I was influenced by nature, which had seemed almost to have died in the drought, but was now burgeoning again, its former distress unremembered in its profusion of greenery and flowers and birds and insects, in the dense golden crops and the rich milk flowing out of the cows. Even my own body had begun to beat to this same pulse, this unthinking rhythm. Turning twelve released in me some chemical reaction that sprang my bones and stretched my skin. In one term I shot up an inch and a half, my knees and hips aching with growing pains. All over my body, hair and sweat and smells oozed and sprouted out, as the shoots and worms and streams had issued from the dry land when the rain fell. Back at school, I saw the same was happening to the other boys, had in some cases been happening for months. We were leaving our old selves behind. Only Derek, who was a few months younger than I was, still steadfastly refused to grow.

I stayed with Derek for a part of each holidays, content to be caught up in the activity of his household. At home, for all the profusion of new life, for all my attempts to forget, I was aware of something old still gnawing away at me. I was conscious of my own listlessness. Even the kitchen was no longer a refuge. Since Margaret's departure, Gatheru had grown even more taciturn, and his face, which had always seemed ageless, had begun to show his years. The rains had failed to rejuvenate him. His skin was wrinkled and dry, and he moved more slowly, his joints arthritic from the cold and damp. Sometimes I would go into the kitchen and find him staring out of the window into the night, as if searching for something he had lost.

Mary's presence reminded me also, prevented me from forgetting. We did not talk much to each other, and when we did, we never directly mentioned Ernest. But on the few occasions we spoke about her home in Luoland, where Ernest also came from, I think we both understood that it was him we were really talking about.

'Have you seen Lake Victoria?' I asked.

'Yes.'

'Did you see the steamboat?'

'Yes,' she whispered. 'I saw it disappear into the horizon.'

'Did you know your mother and father?'

'I know them.'

'Are they both Luo?'

'They are.'

'What does the land look like there?'

She stopped cleaning and narrowed her eyes, remembering. 'If you stand on a hill,' she said, 'you can see all the *shambas* fitting together like the jigsaw puzzle your mother plays in the evenings.'

After a minute, she said, 'How is England?'

'The skies are always grey and everyone wears grey suits,' I told her. 'Except when it snows, then people live in igloos and hunt whales and seals.'

The next term was the first of my last year at the junior school. Pierce and Derek and I were sixth-formers, and we strutted around the school, lording it over the younger boys. One night, Donald produced a new kind of magazine, not a comic, something far more startling. It was full of photographs of women dressed only in their underwear.

'It's just stupid girls,' Derek said. 'I've seen my sisters' tits. They wobble like jelly.'

Some of the boys agreed, but others, like myself, were not so dismissive, and later, when I took my turn to pore over the pages more privately, I was entranced by the way the women's thighs fattened below their underpants, by the flesh dimpling into their belly buttons. My skin tingled and my stomach felt as it did when I clung to the ropes in the gym, my legs crossed tightly to keep me from falling. Filled with both shame and excitement, I began to pay attention to matron's massive calves, to the masters' wives in their pews on Sundays, and the mothers in their cotton dresses when they arrived to take their sons home at the end of term.

One afternoon, in the Christmas holidays, I even found myself watching Mary as she moved about the kitchen, her hips and high bottom sliding beneath the material of her dress, until she looked up, and I turned away, full of guilt, and horrified at what I had allowed myself so idly to do. I was sure that no other white boy in the world would have entered this unthinkable territory, and I waited uneasily for some terrible consequence.

On Boxing Day we went over to the Hadleys. The Chevrolet was in need of some work. It had a big dent in the front bumper from some careless piece of my father's driving, and the gears ground every time he changed up into third. But when we arrived, I was soon caught up in the fevered mood of the party. By that Christmas people were beginning to see an end to the Trouble. The last gangs were being hunted down in the forests and the terrorist violence had a desperation about it, like the lungings of a dying snake. But the prospect of the end of the Trouble brought with it other fears, and I think at that party people were drinking as much to avoid worrying over the future as to forget the past.

Derek had managed to smuggle a bottle of wine away from the servants and had hidden it in the walled garden, and we holed up with a couple of other boys and drank it all. The wine was warm and sour, but I was soon light-headed and full of courage. I walked among the adults, bumping happily against them, and when I found Derek's sister Rose, I stood before her, eyeing her, spellbound by her beauty.

'I love –' I began, and she looked at me, and then giggled gently and opened her mouth. 'I love your teeth.'

She tossed her drink over me and turned away in disgust, and I stumbled back to the walled garden and sat among the flowers, throwing up from time to time and feeling utterly sorry for myself.

I slept in the car on the way home and was helped to bed. When I woke up I was desperately thirsty. I put on my dressing gown and felt my way out into the corridor and began to pad towards the bathroom. Half-way down I realized the light was on in my parents' room, and the door was open a little. I stopped and looked in, about to ask for help. My head felt awful. My mother and father were sitting on the bed and his hand was inside her dress. His face was red and flushed, and I realized that he had been drinking too.

'Philip, please,' she said.

'It's all right,' he whispered. 'Shhh.' His hand snaked around beneath the material.

'No!' she said, her voice breaking.

'What?'

'I can't, I can't,' she whimpered.

My father frowned at her, and then reached out his hand, stroking her hair. 'But it's been two years,' he said softly. 'You need to forget.'

'I know, I know, I'm trying.'

'Well, let's try then.'

'Please, Philip, it's better if we don't. Not now.'

'When then?' he said, more sharply. 'Ever?'

'I don't know,' she sobbed, burying her head in his chest. I watched from the shadows as he held her and stared out over her shoulders, his eyes bloodshot and empty.

A day or two before I was due back at school, I heard that a big monitor lizard had been seen in the lake. I hadn't been down to the lake all holidays. Most of the farm was still out of bounds. But since the Hadleys' party my parents hadn't been paying me much notice anyway. My mother had recovered from one migraine only to relapse almost immediately into another one, and my father had taken to sleeping in the spare room, and keeping away from the house. Most days Mary took his lunch to him in his office.

I picked my way down the path to the lake, taking my time, feeling for the footholds, looking out for plated lizards or skinks or chameleons, wary of *siafu* marching across the track. A little above the lakeside, I stopped in the shade of a thorn tree, beneath the yellow weaver birds flitting in and out of their hanging nests, and scanned the flat surface of the water. Then I descended to the water's edge and walked along beside the reeds, peering in among the long stems, examining the mud on the banks for footprints.

I saw no sign of the lizard, but the next morning, encouraged by my venture, I decided to reacquaint myself with other favourite spots on the farm. I tiptoed from the house and crept down on to the farm and past the farm buildings. It was very hot that day, and I felt almost disembodied, as if I was floating above the earth, looking down on myself. Even if the gangsters caught me, it seemed, it wouldn't matter. Nothing they could do would hurt me. I circled around the farm buildings and then took my old path down to the *shambas*. The squatters were still living in the stockade, but they were working their fields again, and I passed a couple of women bending towards the dry earth, babies on their backs, *shukas* dark red in the sunshine. Some of the families had made efforts to keep up their old homes, hoping to return, but the majority of the huts were falling apart. The thatch had rotted and slipped off the roofs, and birds had built nests in what remained. Grass and weeds were growing up around the huts, poking through holes in the mud walls. When I approached one hut, a duiker dashed out from the shade and bounded away into the bush, dodging and swerving with absurd energy.

On Sundays, I knew, the Africans still attended the church. I had seen them walking away down the hillside in their best clothes, and heard the singing drifting back up a little later. But the schoolteacher had been taken away almost two years earlier and the school remained closed. I stood at the doorway and looked in. There was not much to see. The churchgoers and children had always sat on the floor, and apart from a few church pictures on the walls there was only a wooden lectern, and behind it the blackboard. I remembered when my father had donated this blackboard. Some of the children had been sent up to the house to thank him, with a gift of vegetables. I went in and walked to the board. The ghostly remains of chalk letters from the last lesson were still visible on the black surface and as I looked at them I realized how badly I wanted the school to open up again, the children to return, the Trouble to end. In that moment it seemed to me I knew how to achieve this, how to make my contribution, to begin the process of reconciliation, of putting right what had gone wrong. I understood what I had to do. I had to tell my father about Ernest and the moon.

I turned from the blackboard and ran – through the open doorway of the church, between the empty huts, past the women bending over in the fields and a goat grazing on a thorny bush, up the hill and around the farm buildings, until I slid to a stop in front of my father's office. His door was closed and his curtains were drawn, and normally I would have knocked and waited, for he didn't like to be disturbed if he was working on the accounts. But now, breathlessly, I turned the handle and pushed open the door.

My father was facing away from me and he was bent over, like the women in the fields, only there was no *shuka* stretched over his haunches, no trousers even, except around his ankles. His buttocks were bare and I saw hairs sprouting out from between them like grass from a crack in a rock. Then I realized he was not alone. Someone was beneath him. I saw slender brown calves and the edge of a fleshy hip, flattened against my father's desk. I stared for a moment, while my mind tried to find some harmless explanation. Then I backed away and staggered out, and started running again, up the hill, away from what I had seen, keeping my eyes on the ground, not daring to look back for fear that my father might turn to see who had opened the door, and discover that it was me.

I made first for home, but as I approached the garden, my hot feet thudding into the path, I saw my mother on the veranda, and I swerved away, down towards the lake. I no longer had the strength to run, but gravity helped me stumble down and down until I reached the trees beside the lake and collapsed on the earth. I was burning up. My skin was on fire and my lungs felt like furnaces. Even the surface of the lake glinted with white heat. I thought at any moment I might burst into flame. I closed my eyes and lay down.

When I had caught my breath I opened my eyes again. The water no longer looked hot, but cool and inviting. I took off my shoes and walked out into the shallows. The mud was delicious between my toes. I walked further, up to my knees, my thighs, the water lapping against my shorts, making them cling to my flesh. I stopped and waited resignedly for the itch of a worm as it entered my skin, the claw of a disease tightening around my muscles, my heart. But nothing happened. The water was harmless. All these years my parents had deprived me of this pleasure for no reason.

It was then that I saw the monitor lizard. It was sheltering in the patch of reeds nearest to me, head up, watching me nervously. I stopped and stood still. The lizard lowered its head and slipped into the deeper water, pushing through the reeds and striking out for the far bank, its nostrils above the surface, its tail sweeping back and forth. It was at least three feet long, the tail alone as thick as a man's arm, the muscle taut and gross beneath the wet skin.

Suddenly my gut turned over and I was sick, bent in half, my head throbbing, convulsed by retching until I had emptied my belly and the brown waters I had sullied began to close in and settle again around my legs.

Half a lifetime later, in the weeks after my father's funeral, I found myself waking at night, damp with cold sweat, my hands clenched into fists, my mind gripped by the conviction that the past was not fixed, that the progress of days already lived was not inevitable, and I would struggle as I lay there in those unreal hours to alter the past, to change its course, until I became exhausted and fell back into sleep.

But the boy I was I entertained no such illusions. How could the past be changed when the present could not be controlled, when the future could not be influenced? I submitted myself to my powerlessness as to some suffocating lover. The world was what it was. Returning home from school for the Easter holidays to find Mary departed, I was neither surprised nor disappointed and I did not even ask where she had gone.

If I had I would not have received much of an answer. It was rainy and cold, and the farm was suffering from a pair of plagues, and my parents barely noticed my return. Half the Africans were laid low with a virulent flu and a mystery ailment was killing one of my father's cows every day. My mother, her face weary and drawn, had abandoned her clinic for daily attendance at the stockade, and when my father wasn't trying to coax a dying milker back to life he was sliding through the mud to the veterinary laboratories in town to take in blood samples or collect the latest inconclusive analysis.

In truth, there was little that could be done for the human patients – a few pills, blankets at night and boiled water until the rains and the flu passed – and even less for the cattle. The sick cows had been quarantined, and the rest divided into small groups, but the illness continued to spread. Every morning two or three more cows would be standing apart from the others, ears drooping, flanks heaving, hair standing on end, too sick to eat.

I did not even have the prospect of a temporary escape to the Hadleys to look forward to. Derek and I had drifted apart. There had been no argument or falling out, it was simply that my willingness to follow his lead had dried up, and one day at school I noticed he had a new friend, a new disciple, and it was this friend who had been invited over for the holidays. I wasn't bothered. I sat around the house and read and listened to the radio. The Trouble was now definitely on the wane. There was one brief scare on our farm when, after another stormy night, the body of an old man, a stranger, was discovered hanging from a tree below the *shambas*. But the man was never identified, and if his death was part of the Trouble, then it turned out to be the terrorists' last gasp in our corner of the highlands. On the radio the Trouble had been nudged from the top of the news by the brewing political debate over the future of the colony.

One afternoon, my father was late back from another trip to the veterinary laboratories and when he limped on to the veranda, where my mother and I had just sat down for a cup of tea and a slice of Gatheru's sickly-sweet cake, he was splattered with blood and mud, and one side of his face was swollen out like a beggar with elephantiasis I had seen several times on the streets of Nairobi.

'Philip,' my mother cried, leaping up.

'Don't make a fuss,' my father said. 'Most of it's cow's blood. I hit one on the road. The stupid animal was moving away and turned back at the last minute.'

'Let me look at that.'

'Ow.'

'Sit down,' my mother ordered. 'Here, drink this tea. I'm going to get some hot water.'

'Did you hit the cow?' I asked.

'Hit the bloody thing? I skidded sideways in the mud and the car toppled right on top of it. Not a bad thing really, I might have rolled over completely if the poor bugger hadn't got in the way.' He shook his head and then he looked at me. 'Don't tell your mother that,' he said, trying to smile. 'I was lucky a couple of *watu* came along and helped lift the car off the cow. She tried to stand up, but her leg was broken. Bleeding a lot too.' He reached down to his mud-splattered hip and let his fingers rest on his revolver in his holster. 'She wasn't one of ours. I'll have to find out where she came from.'

It was the most he'd said to me in ages. But then my mother returned, carrying a bowl of hot water and her medical kit, and I left her cleaning his cuts and grazes and walked out to have a look at the Chevrolet.

It was a disaster. Half of one flank was caved in, as if a huge fist had punched it in the midriff, and the whole chassis was skew-whiff, leaning over to one side. I reached out and wiped away some dried mud, and a large flake of green paint came away. The windows down that side and the rear windscreen were all shattered and there was glass and dirt and blood on the seat. Miraculously the front windscreen had stayed in place, through it was so cracked that it looked as if a spider had spun a drunken web across the glass. It was even more of a miracle that my father had been able to drive the car home. I walked all around, running my fingers over its wounded hull, examining every crack and dent, the way my mother examined her patients at the clinic. Eventually, with the light going, I walked back inside.

'I'm not going to kill myself,' my father was saying.

'Well, you'll kill your son.'

'He wasn't even in the car with me.'

'He might have been.'

'Anyway, all this is beside the point. You're just as likely to have a car accident in England as here. More likely probably. There are stray cows on the roads in Worcestershire, and a lot more cars and lorries.'

'I'm not sure I can take any more,' my mother said quietly. 'We're not welcome here. They want us to go.'

'Rubbish,' he replied, exasperation in his voice. 'Does Gatheru want you to go? Do the *watu* you've been looking after in the stockade want you to go? We've got this far. The Trouble is nearly over. We can't leave now.'

A couple of days later a Sikh mechanic came in his truck and towed away the Chevrolet, and my father had to take me to school in the pick-up. At the end of that term, when my father came to collect me, he was driving the Chevrolet again, but a sadly diminished Chevrolet. The Sikh had done what he could to make it roadworthy, but it ran now to a cacophony of rattles and chugs and groans and wheezes. And the mechanic had not worried too much about appearances. He had beaten out the deformed panels with a hammer and repainted them with a shade of green that did not match the rest of the paintwork. The car still leaned slightly to one side, so when it moved it crabbed rather than sailed smoothly down the road.

'It's only a car,' my father said, when I grimaced at the noises it made. 'It's for getting from A to B.'

After that, we barely exchanged a word and I gazed out of the window, my mind blank, all the way home. It was the end of the school year, the end of my time at the junior school, but when we drove away I had not even bothered to look behind me.

Back home, the flu had passed and the cattle disease had disappeared as mysteriously as it had arrived, leaving a quarter of the herd dead but the rest healthy and producing milk as well as ever. The last of the terrorist generals was caught around then and sentenced to death, and I remember thinking through a haze of dullness that the Trouble had taken its last casualty. The squatter families were beginning to move back down to their *shambas* and were building new huts and I was free once again to walk as I liked around the farm. But I had little urge to do so. My old haunts, like the Chevrolet, simply reminded me of happier times. I stayed mostly around the house and even took to sitting on the front steps, watching the kites wheel in the sky and the clouds drift past.

One day, looking up the hill, I saw a tuft of dust appear where the road came over the ridge. Slowly the dust cleared enough to reveal a figure and I realized that I recognized the silhouette, the way it walked, arms held out to the side as if their owner was balancing on a beam. A part of me wanted to stand up, to run up the hill, but I was too wary for that, too full of experience, so I remained on the steps and waited for Ernest to walk slowly down the hill towards me.

'*Habari bwana mjusi*,' he said, coming to a stop beside the Chevrolet, a few feet in front of me. 'Are you still keeping lizards in your shirt?'

I glanced down at my shirt front, and then looked up and shook my head stupidly. Then I said, 'You're not in prison.'

'I got out two days ago.' He was covered in dust and two or three ragged toes were showing through the front of one of an unmatching pair of ancient shoes. 'Did you escape?' I asked. He looked like a fugitive, and I eyed the hillside behind his shoulders, half expecting a police vehicle to appear over the ridge.

His face creased into a dusty smile, and I felt my wariness evaporate and something quicken inside me.

'I can hide you from the police,' I said eagerly. 'There's lots of empty huts down at the *shambas*. I can bring you food –'

'You don't need,' he said. 'I'm finished my sentence. The court gave me two years.'

'But I thought –' I didn't know what I thought, only that I had not expected to see him so soon, to see him again. I looked him over. He seemed shorter, and fatter, or at least less thin, the beginnings of a paunch showing over his trousers. His face was slightly puffy too, as if

138

he was recovering from mumps, and his eyes, which had always been so clear, seemed covered in a film of sticky yellow oil. Red dust was painted like women's make-up on his eyebrows and eyelashes.

'How did you get here?' I asked.

'I walked.'

'You're staying, aren't you?' I said, and the words began to tumble enthusiastically out of me. 'Dad will give you your old job. We haven't got a new mechanic. Even Joshua left. The pick-up's on its last legs and the tractor could do with an overhaul. There's lots of work.'

'I can ask your father.'

'He crashed the Chevrolet,' I said sorrowfully, gesturing towards the car. He followed the direction of my hand and looked down in puzzlement at the vehicle beside him, as if he had not seen it before. 'He hit a cow,' I continued. 'He wasn't hurt badly – Dad, I mean – the cow broke its leg. Dad had to shoot it. A Sikh mechanic patched it up. He didn't do a very good job.'

Ernest looked at the Chevrolet for a while, and then slowly turned back to me.

'*Habari ya* farm?' he said eventually.

'It's all right.'

'Your mother and father?'

'Fine.'

'Gatheru?'

'Fine.'

'How is Mary?'

He said this casually, but his eyes narrowed and I saw them squinting towards the house, as if trying to

139

see through the brickwork, through the windows, black in the sunlight, and I realized that this was the question he had been waiting to ask. I remembered the monitor lizard, its thick, swishing tail, and for a moment I wondered whether Ernest's question about the lizard had been a veiled reference to the monitor lizard, to the events of that day. But then I realized this was impossible.

'She's gone,' I said.

'Gone?'

I nodded, looking away at the hillside.

'Where?'

'I don't know. I was at school.'

His body suddenly began to tremble and he reached out feebly with one hand, and if the Chevrolet had not been there to take his weight I think he might have crumpled to the ground.

He leaned, exhausted, against the car, and his tongue came out and licked at his dry, cracked lips. 'I'll get you some water,' I said, and ran off and came back with a glass. He drank it down in one go and held it out, and I went to fetch him another. When he had drunk this the trembling in his legs and body slowly stopped and his eyes cleared a little.

'Are you hungry?' I asked.

'Hungry?'

'Come on,' I said. 'Let's go to the kitchen and see what Gatheru has cooking.'

That afternoon Ernest moved back into his old room. My father did not seem surprised to see him, and with barely a look at his discharge papers he agreed to take him back. Ernest did not say much.

'But he's a terrorist,' my mother said at supper, when my father told her about Ernest's return.

'If he's a terrorist half the Kikuyu in the colony are terrorists,' my father replied. 'He got caught saying something stupid. Anyway, we need a mechanic.'

The next morning, Gatheru helped to get Ernest's possessions out of storage. The police had gone through Ernest's room and carried away some of his papers and other stuff, and Gatheru had packed what remained into Ernest's suitcase and a couple of boxes. After lunch I slipped out through the kitchen to see how Ernest was doing.

His door was open and he was sitting on the floor in the semi-darkness.

'Are you all right?' I asked.

'My *National Geographic*s,' he whispered.

'What?'

'They took my *National Geographic*s.'

I looked around the room. The suitcase and boxes were open beside him and, while he hadn't unpacked them yet, I could see that he had gone through them.

'The police,' I said. 'Sorry, Ernest.'

'Father gave them to me. I had eleven years, every copy, not one missing. They didn't have to take them.'

He shook his head and gazed at the dark walls, and I said nothing. I understood even then that it was not just the loss of his *National Geographic*s he was mourning. At the time of his arrest his dreams had still been intact, and I imagine that through his imprisonment he had kept hold of these dreams, had told himself that his destiny was only being delayed, as I suppose so many prisoners do. Prisons are full of dreamers. But now that he was back in the real world he was face to face with all he had lost, and at that moment his magazines seemed to encapsulate all of this. I backed out of the room and left him alone.

Over the following days, eating home-cooked food and working under the sun, Ernest's strength slowly returned. His tools had not been taken away and with his kit unrolled at his side he gave the pick-up and tractor overhauls, and began to work on the Chevrolet, promising to fix it up properly when he had time.

'I can find her,' he said one afternoon, lifting his head from beneath the hood of the Chevrolet.

'The gasket's still dirty,' I said, pointing down.

'It won't be like my father.' He was smiling up at the hillside. 'I know her village. She might be with her family, and if she is not they will know where she is.'

'Look here.' I unscrewed the glass cap and held it up, and eventually he lowered his head to see.

I didn't want to talk about Mary, and was worried that someone might say something to Ernest about her and my father. I didn't know what they would say – I certainly didn't have words to describe what I had seen. But if anyone knew anything they kept it to themselves. The Trouble had taught the Africans, had taught all of us, to turn our eyes away, to keep our mouths shut.

My mother wasn't too happy at my spending time in Ernest's company, and if we were visible from the house she often called me in to help her in the garden or with some other task. But if I found him down at the farm buildings, or anywhere outside my mother's territory, I was usually safe.

One Sunday morning, I spotted him walking down

the hill and caught up with him on the path towards the squatters' part of the farm. 'Where are you going?' I asked.

'Just walking,' he said.

We carried on until we were standing on the hillside just above the church. The congregation had already gathered and we could hear the service in progress.

'We can sit here,' Ernest said.

He squatted on the dry earth, and I sat beside him, and for a while neither of us said anything. We listened to the preacher telling a Kikuyu version of a biblical tale.

'We went to church every Sunday in prison,' he said after a time.

'There was a church in the prison?'

'*Ndio*, a prison and a church. Most of the time all we had to read was the Bible. One of the other prisoners refused to go to church so they beat him. He said to them that when the white man came to Africa the black man had the land and the white man had the Bible, but now the white man has the land and the black man has the Bible.' The service had come to an end and the congregation had started singing, an African melody, but the words about Jesus. 'They beat him and took him to church anyway, and when he refused to sing they beat him again.'

'Did they beat you?'

'No,' he said simply. 'I like to sing.'

'But that's not true.'

'It's true,' he protested. 'You've heard me singing.'

'No, I mean about the land. The highlands were empty when the first explorers came, and it was the

Europeans' duty to bring Christianity to heathens. We learned it at school.'

Ernest shrugged. 'It can all be true,' he said. I waited for him to explain, but he said nothing more.

When the singing stopped, I said quietly, 'I would have told them, Ernest. I wanted to.'

'Told them what?'

'What you meant about the moon. I wanted to tell them it wasn't code, that you were really talking about the moon.'

'The moon?' He gave a brief laugh. 'The moon.'

He shook his head slowly, while down below the congregation had started singing again, and when the song floated up the hill towards us it seemed to me that I could see the voices, could see them take wing like birds riding the air currents, and I watched them rise up and up and up, until they disappeared into the emptiness of the unending white sky.

CHAPTER SIX

Through that dry season, Ernest slipped back into his old routine: driving and mechanics during the day, and sitting on his step at dusk. His face lost some of its puffiness, and one day he even laughed the way I remembered, his ears twitching, his nose wrinkling, his eyes swallowed up by the bellows of his purple cheeks. And if he forgot my birthday that July, and the Chevrolet never quite got the magical restoration he had promised, then I shrugged off my disappointment. *Don't expect*, I told myself. *Don't hope.* I understood now that nothing was ever as good as it promised, that nothing lasted.

One morning my mother sent Ernest off with a shopping list for the *dukas*. He was expected back by three at the latest, but when my father came up to the house shortly after six Ernest had still not returned.

'Perhaps he broke down,' my mother suggested.

'Broke down? Ernest?'

They looked at each other. Embers seemed to flare up between them.

'I'll go,' my father sighed.

He fetched a couple of men, and took the pick-up,

and set off into the night. I was in bed when they returned, two or three hours later, with the Chevrolet, but without Ernest.

I got out of bed and opened my door, and listened to my parents' voices. 'He was drunk,' my father said.

'Drunk?'

'In one of those tin shacks behind the shops. He had that bleary face they get. He wouldn't listen to reason. Wouldn't say anything.'

'He seems to have done the shopping,' my mother said, rustling paper. 'Everything's here.'

'It was in the car.'

'Philip, I don't like it.'

'Yes, I know, I'll deal with it. You know, I'd never have thought it of Ernest.' There was silence, then he sighed. 'I expect he'll crawl back tomorrow with a hangover, full of contrition – they usually do.'

Ernest hadn't crawled back by the time I woke in the morning. I pulled my clothes on and went straight through the kitchen to his room and knocked on his door. There was no answer. I tried the handle and the door opened. A few of his clothes were scattered around. There was nothing on the wall. He had done nothing to the room since coming back. He hadn't even finished unpacking his suitcase and boxes.

I finally spotted him from the front windows around noon, walking down the track. When he went round the side of the house I followed him from inside and watched him through the kitchen window. He went straight to the tap and scooped water into his mouth with his hands. Then he splashed more on his face. It trickled down his shirt, mingling with the beer stains and stickiness and dust. Then he went into his room.

My father turned up half-way through the afternoon and I watched again from the kitchen as he banged on Ernest's door until it opened and Ernest came out, bare-chested, rubbing his eyes and ears.

'Well?' my father said.

Ernest blinked at him.

'You leave the shopping rotting in the hot car. You're hours late. You're drunk. I have to come down in the night to fetch my own car. What have you got to say for yourself?'

Ernest's blinking had stopped, but he was looking my father over now, as if seeing him for the first time, or at least seeing him anew, and I could tell it made my father uneasy.

'Come on, Ernest,' my father said, trying to be placatory, showing Ernest the palms of his hands. 'I've given you a chance. I believe in giving people a chance. Most farmers wouldn't have taken you back, not after –'

'What about university?' Ernest's words were slow and quiet, but they cut across my father's speech, and my father jerked back in surprise.

'What?'

'You said when the Emergency was over you would help me get to university. The Emergency is over.'

At this it was my father's turn to stare. Eventually he gave out a humourless bark. 'Be serious, Ernest. That was before you got yourself sent to prison. Do you think even if I wanted to help you the university would take you now? A convicted terrorist?'

For a moment more Ernest looked at my father. Then he nodded slowly and turned back into his room.

That night I listened through the door to my parents discussing Ernest's fate until I couldn't stand it any longer. I pushed open the door and stood there in my pyjamas. 'But, Dad, he was innocent,' I said.

'What were you doing out there?'

'I want a drink.'

'You shouldn't listen outside doors,' my mother said.

'But it's not fair, he was innocent.' I didn't know where I'd got this word, probably from a film I'd seen or a book I'd read, but it had been echoing around my head all day.

'Innocent?' my father said. 'He was drunk.'

'No, innocent about the moon.'

'The moon?'

'Yes, he told me about the moon ages ago, about people flying to the moon. He knows about science and engines, Dad. Cars and trains and aeroplanes. Bridges too, and buildings and all that stuff. He reads all these magazines. He says people are really going to travel to the moon. He says maybe the land will be good for crops and there will be room for everyone to farm. He told me about the moon before the Trouble even began.'

My father narrowed his eyes. 'Why didn't you tell me this before?'

'I wanted to, but no one would listen.'

'Look, I don't know whether any of this is true or not. You've always paid too much attention to Ernest. That's another reason for letting him go.' His face softened slightly. 'Anyway, whether he was innocent or guilty is beside the point. That was then and this is now. He hasn't left me any choice.'

'But, Dad –'

'I'll write him a letter of recommendation. I shouldn't really. It might help him get a job in one of the Sikh garages.'

I opened my mouth to protest again, but I was too late – I was always too late.

In the morning, my father went to dismiss Ernest. But he was too late as well. Ernest was already gone. He had slipped out in the night, taking his suitcase with him, leaving the rest of his stuff neatly packed in a box, stacked in the corner of the otherwise immaculate room, as if only in deciding to leave had he discovered enough purpose to tidy up.

I woke with a burning in my side. I tried to get up, but the movement almost made me sick, so I lay back again and eyed the pain suspiciously through the sheets, as if I was merely a witness to its intensifying. Eventually, my mother came to see why I wasn't up and ran her fingers over my belly.

'I think it's appendicitis,' she said, showing my father, when he had been fetched from the dairy. 'We should take him to hospital. It might burst.'

'What's pendicitis?' I whispered. 'What might burst?'

On the way to the car I was sick, and the pain subsided a little. In fact, it can't have been very bad, for I remember that drive down to the city almost with pleasure. I curled up in the back, next to my mother, a blanket tucked around me, drifting in and out of sleep, cocooned by the irresponsibility of the ill. It was out of my hands now. There was nothing I could do about my pain or anything else. Other people would take care of me. Other people would take care of the world.

At the hospital, the doctor agreed with my mother's diagnosis. 'It's going down, but it could flare up again at any time. He ought to have it out. We might as well do it today.'

I surfaced from the anaesthetic with the burning and sickness gone, only a tugging and cramp in my belly. I spent a week in the hospital, sleeping and watching the nurses on the ward, and reading the newspaper, whose pages were full of the forthcoming election to the colony's Legislative Council.

The day I should have been starting my first term at senior school, my parents came to drive me home. The doctor had taken my stitches out, and I walked out of the ward. The doctor told my parents to bring me back in a week's time. At home, I lay on the veranda, watching the hoopoes and the paradise flycatchers instead of nurses. In hospital, I had thought of my cut, tender beneath its dressing, as a trophy, as something manly. But now when I slid my hand down over my belly all I felt was an ugly welt, hot to the touch.

Most of the boys from my junior school had moved on to the same senior school, and I tried to imagine what they were doing. Sometimes I thought about Ernest.

When I had been home a week, my father drove me down to Nairobi to see the doctor. I sat slightly hunched. If I was too upright, the bumps pulled at my scar and set my teeth on edge. But when we slowed down to drive through the *dukas*, I straightened up and stared out of the open window. We still called this place the *dukas*, but it was more of a shanty town now, and it was still growing, swelling with families returning from the forests and reserves, and with the first of the detainees released from the camps. Young men, no longer frightened of being picked up by the police, but without jobs, or land to work, hung about on the main street, talking, scheming, watching the cars go by. We were almost through the settlement when I saw a last such group. I glanced at them sideways, not wanting to catch a bloodshot eye, and we had almost passed before I realized one of them was Ernest. He was standing slightly apart from the others, but he looked up as we passed, and when I raised my hand I thought he saw me, for his hand began to rise too. But I could not be sure, for at that moment he passed out of the frame of the window and by the time I turned painfully round to look back the car was picking up speed towards the clear road ahead, and the dust behind us obscured the view.

On the way back I scanned the street again for Ernest, and over the following days, whenever a car went down to the *dukas*, I found an excuse to go with. But I saw no sign of Ernest. He was gone. For all I knew he might have been only a few yards back, in one of the shacks or bars behind the shops. But that was far enough. Once he stepped off the main street he was swallowed up by the hinterland, by the great African vastness that stretched away in every direction, to the deserts, to the forests, to the mountains, beyond my reach, beyond my comprehension.

*

I malingered at home, complaining of pains, weakness, fever. I wasn't in any hurry to recover. Being ill suited my state of mind; I had no desire to engage with life. The only thing that managed to rouse my interest was the election campaign, and that barely seemed to belong to our world. Every day the *Standard* ran profiles of three or four of the candidates, and I liked seeing what they looked like in the accompanying photographs. A few you could tell were farmers, but most had dressed up for the photographer in collars and ties, and combed their hair, and they stared out seriously from the newspaper like actors from old black and white movies. Even the names of their parties – United, Empire – sounded like the names of cinemas.

But as I read more, I became more interested in the mechanics of the election, in the issues. I suppose I was bored, I wanted something to occupy my mind without touching my heart, and politics reminded me of maths, absorbing within its own edges, its own angles and equations, but unlikely to have much application to my own life.

In the history books, for those years are history now, I expect that election is marked down as the first in the colony in which Africans had a vote. But only a few Africans actually qualified for the franchise and just three or four of the seats were reserved for African candidates, and at the time the *Standard* was much more concerned with the European ballot. In strict terms, this was only a formality. The elections were to the colony's Legislative Council and the majority of seats were still appointed by the Governor. And anyway, if the Council got uppity, the Governor could always override it. But to the European settlers, with mutiny on their minds, the election was seen as a referendum on the future of the colony.

Every day I read the latest interviews with the candidates. These men were not professional politicians, and though most represented one or other party they did not stick to any party line. They were farmers, frontiersmen who prided themselves on their fierce independence and strong morals. Each had his own ideas on the issues of the day: land division, the colour bar, the tax burden, schools and hospitals, immigration, the Indian question. But the heart of the matter, the central issue, divided them clearly on either side of a thick line. They were either for multiracialism – for involving Africans in government – or against. This was not about African independence, about black rule. It was about white rule or beige rule, but for those months those two colours seemed at opposite ends of the spectrum.

One morning I opened the paper and saw a photograph of Captain Alec Smith. He was against, and he was standing in our constituency. The paper also said there was to be a debate that weekend between him and his opponent, Cedric Watling, on a rugby field a couple of miles below the *dukas*.

'Who do you support, Dad?' I asked that night.

'Support?' he said, looking up from his accounts. 'When I was your age I supported Pompey.'

'Who's that?'

'Portsmouth Football Club.'

'I mean which candidate do you support? Who are you going to vote for, Smith or Watling?'

He didn't answer. He didn't seem to approve of my

interest in the election and several times when he saw me studying the political articles in the paper he told me to go out into the fresh air, or read something more healthy.

'Well,' I said, 'I'm not going to make my mind up until the meeting at the rugby field.'

He looked up now. 'And who says you are going?'

'But, Dad!'

'If you're not fit enough for school, you're not fit enough to go to some political rally.'

'But I'm better now. Almost completely.'

'Then you can get off your bottom and help around the house. And next week you are going to school.'

'But can I go to the meeting?'

'We'll see,' he said. 'You can start by washing the car in the morning. It's filthy.'

The next day I filled a bucket with soapy water and took it outside. Physically I was completely recovered. My muscles no longer pulled and the scar had settled down. It was only inertia that was keeping me inactive. I dipped a cloth into the bucket and started slopping the water over the Chevrolet. Green rivulets ran through the caked dust. It was weeks since the car had been cleaned, let alone oiled or repaired. I dunked the cloth back in the bucket and stood there, remembering, while water dripped from my hand on to the earth below.

'What do you say, Ernest?' I whispered finally. 'We can fix the old girl up. A bit of work and she'll be like new.'

Suddenly, I was inspired. I opened the boot and looked in. Ernest's cleaning box was still there. I took it out. It was full of tins and brushes and shammies.

'We'll do the inside first,' I said. 'Like we used to.' I began by wiping clean the leather seats and the chrome handles and the mock wood dashboard – working carefully around the cigarette lighter, the choke, the throttle, the lights, the dials, the glove box, the radio, the ivory switch for the windscreen wipers. Then I wiped the rubber mat by the pedals and brushed the carpet in the back. When the leather was dry, I opened the tin of leather feed and rubbed it gently in until the leather began to shine. 'All right, Ernest? Let's do the outside now. You start at that end and I'll start at this, we'll meet in the middle. Come on now, we haven't got all day.' I washed the outside and rubbed the windows and chrome dry with a shammy. Then I began to apply polish to the paint.

'What's taking so long?' my father asked, standing in the doorway.

'Ernest and I are making her shine.'

'Ernest?'

For a moment his question stumped me. But then I realized that I should play along with him. 'I'm doing it the way Ernest showed me.'

'All right,' he said. 'It looks good.'

I went back to work. When I reached a patch of rust or bubbled paint I healed the wounds with my fingers. Finally the paintwork was completed and I opened up the tin of chrome polish, and finished off the chrome, buffing it up until it shone as it had in its early days. I stood back and admired my work.

'A real Master de Luxe,' I whispered. 'Well done, Ernest. You can start university tomorrow.'

*

In the end all of us went to the meeting, as did most of the Europeans from our part of the highlands. It wasn't often we had a chance to gather all together. Dozens of cars were parked at the edge of the field and one or two families with young children had even decided to make an occasion of the day, and had arrived early with picnics and drinks. I stood by the Chevrolet watching the adults talking. It was term-time so the only other children were babies and toddlers. Out on the field a couple of young men were kicking a ball about, and I watched it making high arcs against the bleached red of the escarpment behind and the white of the sky above.

'Hello,' a voice said behind me.

I turned round. 'Oh, Derek.'

'You had an operation.'

'Appendix,' I said. 'It had to come out. It might have burst.'

'You look all right now.'

'I am, almost. I'll be coming to school next week.' Then I realized Derek should have been at school. 'What are you doing here?'

'Helping my father,' he said casually. 'He organized all this, you know. I came home for the weekend. Dad wanted me to hear what Alec Smith has to say.'

'He came to our house.'

'My Dad's his agent, actually.'

He stood with his hands on his hips, as confident as ever. But looking down at him I saw how small he was. While I had shot up that year, he had barely grown an inch, and there was something in his small frame that undermined his assurance, as if his own stunted body was mocking his adult airs.

'What happened to your car?' he said suddenly.

I turned and looked at the Chevrolet, dappled in the light coming through the trees. 'I fixed it up,' I said proudly.

'No,' he said, giving me a withering glance. 'I mean it's a mess. Look at it.'

I stepped away in surprise and examined the Chevrolet again. It was true. All I had done was clean the car and now, after the drive down, it was splattered again with dust. The panels the Sikh had beaten out were pockmarked, as if an automatic rifle had sprayed soft bullets against the metal. And the dappling I had noticed before was as much due to the unmatching layers of green paint as to any effect of the light. The whole body of the car leaned precariously to one side. It was crippled, lame, like my father. Somewhere inside me, I felt a flutter of foreboding. Derek, I realized, was not the only boy making a fool of himself.

Despite myself, I still said, 'We're getting a Cadillac next.' But fortunately Derek had turned away and was watching people moving out on to the field.

We followed them to the rugby posts at one end. Some of the women had brought folding chairs, but most simply sat on the ground, while their men stood behind. There must have been almost 200 Europeans in all, as well as a handful of *askaris*, and another twenty or so Africans, looking on curiously from the edge of the field. I saw my mother standing beside my father, and waved at her, but she was looking the other way. 'Let's sit here,' Derek said, beckoning me to the front.

'That's Watling,' Derek said, pointing at a man mopping his forehead with a crumpled handkerchief. 'My

Dad says he's soft in the head.' There were five or six men, including Captain Smith and Mr Hadley, sitting behind a big picnic table. Then another man, whose name I didn't catch, stood up and said a few words, before introducing Mr Watling as the first speaker.

Mr Watling had taken off his jacket, but his collar seemed stiff about his neck and there were dark patches under his arms. He pushed his glasses up his nose and blinked out at us.

'Ladies and gentlemen,' he began, his voice thin and frail beneath the wide sky and the field stretching away to the escarpment. 'I represent your interests. I am a farmer and my livelihood lies in this land just as all your livelihoods do.'

'Dad says he's a rotten farmer,' Derek whispered.

Mr Watling spoke for a while about his hopes for the highlands and the support he envisaged the government giving to farmers and any new settlers, and the crowd listened politely. Then he said, 'But we must accept we are not alone here. This is European land, yes. But it is also African land. The African is not going to go away, and I don't think there is anyone here who would want him to. If he did, who would work on our farms? Who would work in our houses? We need Africans as much as we need cattle and crops.' He paused here and mopped his brow again, keeping the handkerchief in his hand. 'We need Africans. They are our already our partners, our junior partners. Let me assure you, I am not proposing to give away the leadership of this colony –'

'You'd better bloody not,' someone muttered.

'But at the same time we have brought Africans on, we have educated them, we have encouraged them to develop themselves. We cannot pretend otherwise. There are already African doctors, African engineers. We must take these people into account. We must allow them responsibility. That is why I say we must have Africans, and Indians, in government. The only hope for this country is multiracialism.'

'How much is Whitehall paying you?' someone yelled out.

'Please,' Mr Watling said, horror on his face.

'Enough of that.' It was Mr Hadley, suddenly standing up. 'There's no need for insults. We want honest political debate.'

'Thank you,' Mr Watling said. Drops of sweat had collected on his forehead and I watched one swell until it broke, and a trickle ran down his nose until he dabbed it away with his handkerchief. 'What is multiracialism?' he continued. 'It means sharing this wonderful land. But it doesn't have to mean sharing everything. There should not be a colour bar, but a culture bar is quite natural. There is no reason we should have to share our schools or hospitals or clubs.'

'What about toilets?' a woman's voice called out, to hoots of laughter.

'Yes,' a man joined in. 'A toilet bar. Squatting over a hole disqualifies you.'

'Or squatting on the seat like a bloody Hindi!'

When the laughter had died down, Mr Watling carried on, but he had lost what control he had established over the crowd. There was no more shouting out, but every once in a while someone would whisper 'toilet bar' and laughter would ripple through the crowd.

Every time this happened, Mr Watling shook his hand in agitation, and the handkerchief, which he had apparently forgotten, waved like a white flag. Eventually he finished and sat down, and I felt my own breath returning in relief that his ordeal was over.

Captain Smith was now introduced, and he stepped forward, smiling broadly.

'My friend here,' he began, gesturing to Mr Watling, 'thinks we can have African ministers in our government but not allow the same Africans into our schools and hospitals.' He paused and opened his palms to us. 'Is this possible? I think not. Once an African is my political senior, how can I not invite him into my children's school, my club, my home? How can I refuse him if he wants to marry my daughter?'

There were a few gasps and a single bark of laughter, but most of us were silent, gripped by his words.

'And why not?' he continued. 'Why not? I am all for it. Let us share everything. Our homes, our schools, our hospital beds, these highlands. But –' and here he stopped, his eyes roving around his audience – 'let us do it when the African is ready for it, when he has earned it. When he has merited it.'

'That'll be the day!' a voice cried out.

'Perhaps,' he said in response. 'Perhaps. We shall have to see. That is not something we can decide. None of us can know when the African will be ready to take responsibility for his own affairs. For our affairs.' He paused again here, allowing the meaning of his words to sink in. 'In the meantime, I am utterly against the quotas the Governor wants, that Mr Watling here wants. What is the point of reserving places in government for Africans if they do not merit such places? We might as well dress a monkey in a suit. I say this approach is disastrous and insulting – insulting to the African as much as to us. Forget multiracialism. Think non-racialism. I am not against the African having three seats on LegCo. I would be happy for him to have ten, or twenty – if he merits them. But if he does not, give him none. Merit and ability determine a man's right to a position of influence. Merit and ability, and these alone.' By now he was beating the air with his hand in time with his words. 'And if that means that Europeans continue to control the politics and economics of this colony, then that is only right and proper because we are best suited to government at this moment in history.'

'And every other moment!'

'Bravo!'

The applause was so strong that Captain Smith had to hold up his hand for silence. 'I am not saying that the African, as well as the Arab and the Indian, does not have a part to play in our future. He does. My own houseboys are almost part, are part, of my family. I don't doubt there's a man or woman here who does not feel the greatest affection for Africans they've known for many years. But their skills are best expressed when directed by Europeans. To that end we advocate schools with an emphasis on practical education . . .'

He went on to list the details of his programme, almost every one of which drew further approval, and when he was finally finished the farmers' big hands met in powerful applause.

The meeting was now open to the floor, and several

men stepped forward with comments. One was a very old man who leaned on a cane. 'I came here in 1910,' he said, his voice surprisingly strong. 'There were still natives then who had never seen a white man. When we built our first house we had to close our windows at night because of the noise of dancing and singing from the African huts. They were simple people. Happier than us, I don't doubt. And what has the government done? It has used our taxes from our hard labour to pay for schools that educate Africans to want what they can never have. To be grumpy and resentful. If you ask me, that is nothing less than unChristian.'

'He's right,' a man said. 'It's us who pay all the taxes. They don't pay a penny but want all the services.'

Almost all the voices were for Captain Smith and each new piece of testimony seemed to echo what had gone before, until it seemed there was nothing more to say. The candidates looked out at us, ready to stand up, one to accept the handshakes of victory, the other to slink off in defeat. The chairman began to rise to call the meeting to a close, but half-way up he stopped and sat down again, gesturing for one more offering from the floor.

'I have listened . . .' To my surprise, I realized this was my father's voice. I turned and saw him stepping forward from the crowd. 'I have listened to what has been said today,' he continued, 'and I can appreciate what Captain Smith says about merit and ability. I grew up, as I know others did, in the Depression in England, where it was position . . .' His words drifted up into the hot air, and I examined him, looking at him through the eyes of the crowd. His face was creased with reluctance, his big hands were interlaced, his eyes were focused above the bar of the rugby posts. 'You cannot talk about merit,' he was saying when I caught his thread again, 'without talking about opportunity. People need, even Africans –'

'So what do you mean?' someone called out.

'What I mean –'

'Speak up,' another man demanded, and the crowd hushed as people strained to hear my father's words, curious, perhaps to hear such a private man speak his mind. 'What I mean,' my father repeated, louder this time, 'is that if we want the Africans to come along with us, then they need a stake in the future. Captain Smith was very persuasive . . .' He paused here, his brows furrowed as he searched for the right words. 'But this is not a black and white issue.' A few dry laughs greeted this, but my father carried on, apparently unaware of the pun he had made. 'We can give Africans a stake without giving them our daughters . . .'

'But we must give you *our* daughters?'

This was a new voice. My father had paused again here, and these words rang out in the silence, filling the gap he had left. I turned round. Others were turning too. Everyone had heard the interruption – everyone, that is, except my father, who was concentrating so hard that he could hear only the words inside his head.

'Or give up our land,' my father continued painfully. 'But it is our duty –'

'This is your duty?'

This time even my father heard, and he lowered his head and squinted into the audience in surprise. The crowd was stirring, heads turning, a murmur spreading across the field. I stood up, straining to see, trying to place the voice, curiously familiar, but also somehow out of place, foreign in this gathering. From nearby an angry squawk went up and someone cried, 'What the devil!' Voices were raised. A man said, 'Grab the cheeky bugger.' But no one was grabbed and, as if by magic, the crowd of white people parted to reveal, standing in a circle of space, two Africans, a man and a woman, Ernest and Mary.

'This is your duty?' Ernest said. It was Ernest who had been speaking, Ernest whose voice had been both so familiar and so incongruous. It rang inside my head now, and I heard again its strangeness in this white setting, its African-ness. I heard what the crowd heard: its cheek, its threat.

Something was called out, and two or three of the nearest farmers began to move towards Ernest, their heavy shoulders hunched like hyenas. In comparison, Ernest seemed tiny and vulnerable, and Mary beside him even smaller. But suddenly, in one movement, thrusting up his hands, Ernest stopped the farmers dead. In his hands, held into the air, was a baby.

A baby. My heart soared. A baby. It was our baby, my mother's baby, the one we had lost. Ernest had found it. He had brought it back to us. The farm would be happy again. My mother and father would love each other. Ernest would win back my father's favour, would earn a place at university. I imagined the headline in the paper: ENGINEER-TO-BE FINDS LOST BABY. All this passed through my head in the second before I realized that the baby could not be ours, could not be my mother's. Its face, blinking out of its swaddling, was not white. It was brown – though oddly not nearly as dark as Ernest or Mary. A pale brown, a beige.

'To give us this child?' Ernest said, holding the baby even higher. One of the farmers who had advanced towards him, a man named Roberts or Russell, took another step forward, but then hesitated, and looked back to my father. Others looked too, following Ernest's eyes, for there was no doubting to whom Ernest was addressing his questions. Roberts or Russell remained poised, waiting for my father to give him some sign, some indication that this upstart African should be ejected, should be thrown out on his heels for his cheekiness. But my father did nothing, and in his silence was an admission that gave Ernest a terrible authority over the men who all his life had held sway over him.

Perhaps we might all have stood there for ever, in silence, transfixed by the child, which gurgled happily in the sunlight, had it not been for the African *askaris*. They, it seemed, were unaffected by Ernest's power. They moved forward and I saw hands take hold of Ernest and Mary. The spell was broken. Suddenly Ernest's face creased with some awful anguish. Still staring at my father, his lips moved, and I could see he was trying to say something more, but either no words came or the words were lost in the noise that erupted at that moment. Then Ernest and Mary were gone, and the gap in the crowd closed after them like a sea.

As one, the farmers and their wives turned now to look at my father, to hear what he had to say, still hoping for a denial, for an attempt at a denial at least, however belated. But my father made no sound. His big fingers were still linked together and his mouth was half open, as if he was trying to remember what he had been about to say when he had been so rudely interrupted.

Sometimes as these memories pass so clearly before my eyes, before all my senses, I wonder whether the forgetting I accomplished at such a young age had the effect of burying the past intact, interring it as effectively as a Pharaoh in a tomb, so that now, when I have finally come to recall, it is simply a case of excavating my boyhood in one piece, unspoiled, unlooted. But then I come to a part of my story where my memory is uncertain, or incomplete, or does not make sense, and I am forced to accept that I cannot simplify everything, that I cannot always make the world the ordered place I want it to be.

These past months I have turned that day over and over in my mind, but as hard as I try I cannot find my mother. The last image I have is of her looking in the other direction when I waved to her, before the meeting began. After that, nothing. I cannot see her when my father spoke. I cannot see her when Ernest and Mary appeared through the crowd. I cannot see her in the car on the way home, though somehow we got home, for I remember my father telling me that my mother was in bed with a migraine, that she was not to be disturbed.

Leaving my father staring at the walls of the living room, I went out on to the veranda. I considered walking around the house to the servants' quarters on the off chance that Ernest and Mary had come back, that their presence at the meeting was an attempt to win back their old jobs. But I decided against it. The *askaris* had taken them away. Ernest was probably heading back to prison. I didn't feel like staying around the house, though, so I walked across the lawn and took the path through the flowerbeds and down the hillside, past the farm buildings, towards the *shambas*.

I had not been this way for weeks – not since the Sunday Ernest and I had sat listening to the singing from the church – and I was surprised by how much had changed. The squatters had moved back down on to their land, and were living in new huts they had constructed on their *shambas*. The old huts, which had stood for so long like silent reminders of the Trouble, were gone. Women were pounding maize again in front of their doors. Children were playing in the dust. Chickens scrabbled for scraps. A goat gnawed absent-mindedly at its rope. Blue smoke curled out of the roofs.

The women nodded and smiled. A gang of small children ran forward and stood watching me, arms flopped over each other's shoulders, hands held in hands. '*Mzungu*,' one of them whispered. '*Mzungu*.' They fell about giggling.

It was getting towards the end of the day and the light was beginning to fade. I turned and started to walk back up the hill. When I reached the church, I stopped and looked down the slope towards the valley far beneath. If I ran fast enough, I thought, and held my arms out, I would be able to take off and fly above the world. Nothing had ever seemed so simple, so enticing. I began to take in deep breaths, preparing myself.

'I thought you'd be down at the lake.' My father was walking towards me. 'I looked for you at the lake.' His brows were still knitted. His face had not lost its look of puzzlement.

'Everyone's back on their *shambas*,' I said. 'Everything is going to be all right now.' I was suddenly filled with a wild optimism, and I would have laughed out loud if my father had not looked so serious.

'Come on,' he said. 'It's getting dark.'

We turned and began to walk up the narrow path, my father a pace ahead of me. We were within sight of the house when we heard the sound. It wasn't as loud as I would have imagined, or particularly startling. It was simply a soft thud, like a brick being dropped on to a damp lawn.

We walked on a few steps, and then my father began to run, throwing his weight on to his good leg and dragging the bad one after him, his trailing foot scuffing up tiny clouds of dust.

PENUMBRA

I pressed my face to the window and watched the concrete and grass judder past until they fell away. For a few seconds I thought we could not possibly make it, that our weight would drag us down, that the effort was shaking the aeroplane apart, but then the wings tipped and there was only blue sky in the window. The plane was a Lockheed Constellation, with a silver body, four propellers and three tail planes.

We stopped three or four times: Entebbe, Khartoum, some ghostly strip in North Africa in the middle of the night. At one of these, when my neighbour got up to stretch his legs, I picked up his newspaper and, turning over the pages, chanced across a paragraph:

Terrorism blamed for suicide
A farmer's wife shot herself with the gun she had kept by her bedside in case of attack by terrorists. The coroner was told she had used the same gun to protect herself when a lone terrorist broke into her farm and threatened her with a *panga*. She had suffered from illness ever since.

Towards dawn, the pilot announced that we were over the Mediterranean and approaching Europe. Silently, without my noticing, Africa had slipped out from beneath the aircraft's belly and disappeared behind us.

My father followed two months later, having packed up the house, sold the vehicles, made arrangements for the servants and squatters, and left the disposal of the farm in the hands of an agent. Having wanted only to stay in Africa, he was back in England, while my mother, who had longed for this return, had been left behind for ever, buried in the red African earth she could not learn to love.

We spent that Christmas in Worcester, with my grandparents: a cold Christmas, full of long silences. One week it snowed, and with the neighbours' children I went tobogganing on the Malvern Hills, hurtling down cold white slopes in the new coat my father had bought me – to keep, as I saw it, what was left of Africa's warmth inside me. In the New Year my father found a job in the south of England, and we moved away. We did not talk about my mother. My father never mentioned her funeral. More had happened to us than we had words to discuss. So we buried the past along with my mother, and set about forgetting.

I studied hard at school and won a place at one of the new universities, and within a month of passing my final examinations I had settled into a job with prospects and a pension plan. One weekend, shortly before I left home for good, my father took me for a walk in the park near our house and offered me a rare piece of advice. 'All you can be sure of in life,' he said, 'is that people will let you down. Trust only yourself, rely only

on yourself, and you will never be caught by surprise.'
Now I can see that, in his own oblique way, he was
referring back to Africa, to the past we had left behind,
and that for all his silence he had not forgotten, though
all he had to express was this dour bitterness. But at the
time I took his words at face value. I was twenty-two
years old and I wanted nothing more of surprises, and I
let these words sink into me in the way I suppose the
faith of religious fathers sometimes sinks without question into their sons. I took what he said as gospel, as if
there was no other way of looking at life, and it was not
until he died, all these years later, that I began to see by
what arbitrary laws I have lived my years. We cannot
escape what has gone before. The past awaits us all,
somewhere up ahead.

In the weeks that followed my father's funeral, I
spent my evenings and weekends sorting through his
possessions. The few good pieces of furniture I arranged for an auction house to collect; the rest of his
stuff I took in boxes to Oxfam. When the house was
empty I gave the key to an estate agent and told him to
call me when he had sold it. I went back to my own
empty flat and sat in my armchair, looking again at my
father's bank papers, at the standing order in the name
of Ernest Shianyisa.

When morning came, I called my office and told
them I was taking a holiday. They did not object: it
was years since I had been away for more than a day
or two. There was no one else to tell. I had not
always been alone, not always celibate, but none of
the women with whom I had formed liaisons had
ever stayed for very long. I was never the one to end

relationships, but somehow I was always responsible, the one to feel let down, to withdraw in fear. I packed a small bag, locked my door and drove to Heathrow airport, where I bought a ticket on the first plane to Nairobi: just as sixty years earlier my father had purchased a passage on the first ship out of Portsmouth.

When I had travelled after my mother's death from Africa to England, the flight had seemed endless and absolute – a journey of such immensity that it could only possibly be made once – and I had accepted, without question, that I would never set foot in Africa again. But now, after a meal and a couple of drinks and a few hours' sleep, here I was waking to see the brown face of Africa rising to meet me. I felt light-headed, disorientated, unsure whether the turmoil inside me was anticipation or regret – like an old man who discovers that the woman he loved long ago, but believed was dead, is in fact still alive and has been living for years in the next town.

It was early in the morning when a taxi dropped me off in the centre of Nairobi. At first nothing was familiar. But slowly I began to see buildings I remembered, to recognize the old town in the face of the new city. I walked among the people hurrying to work, carrying my bag, remembering shops, cinemas, hotels, fending off the street vendors with Swahili that rose unbidden to my lips. Finally I searched out the bank where my father's standing order had been sent each month. I waited in a queue for the best part of an hour, and when I reached the front the young man behind the glass listened to what I had to say, and turned away.

For a minute or two I thought he was ignoring me, that I might be denied the information I needed. I had no rights here. I was a tourist, a visitor. This was not my country.

But then I was ushered through a door, and offered a seat and a cup of tea by a fat, smiling woman, who might have been Margaret's granddaughter.

'Every month for many years that money has come,' she said. 'Your father was very generous.'

'Yes.'

'You will continue sending?' she smiled.

'I hadn't ... Yes, of course I will. But you see, it's been so many years and I was hoping to meet Mr Shianyisa.'

'Of course, of course. Now let me see, all I can tell you is that we have been transferring this money to our branch in Kisumu. Mr Shianyisa must live in that place. If you go there the manager will be able to help you. I can send him a message.'

'Yes, I'll do that. Thank you. Thank you very much. You have been very kind.'

She smiled, as if her help was both nothing and every-thing, as if every day she played a part in changing people's lives.

I walked down the road to the bookshop, and then found an empty table among the backpackers and middle-aged tourists at the hotel where my father and mother and I had eaten lunch together all those years ago, and spread out the map I had just purchased. I followed the line with my finger to Kisumu. The road took me past Naivasha, Gilgil, Molo, Kericho. The names echoed in my memory. I folded up the map and walked next door to a car-hire shop, and by noon I was driving out of town up the hill towards the highlands.

I stopped for lunch at a small hotel on a tea estate and sat on the veranda, watching the women working in the fields, their clothes bright against the deep green of the tea bushes. I had planned to stop at another hotel for the night, but each time I saw a sign I pushed on and by late afternoon I realized I could make it to Kisumu that same evening. It was dark when I reached the outskirts of the town and I followed the road until I came to the lake shore. I stopped the car. I had seen the Indian Ocean in the east, but I had never seen this inland sea in the west, and I stared out into the night, unable to find where the lake ended and the black sky began.

A sign pointed the way along the lakeside to a hotel and I parked the car and walked up to the desk.

'Are you here on holiday, sir?' the young man said.

'Holiday?' I said. The word sounded strange, foreign. 'Yes, I suppose I am.'

He smiled at me and I suddenly had an urge to open my heart, to share my quest with someone.

'Actually, I'm looking for someone. His name is Ernest Shianyisa.'

'Mr Shianyisa. I know him well, sir.'

'You do?'

'Yes, he's the Chief Engineer.'

'Engineer?'

I blinked at him and leaned forward and put both my hands on the counter.

'Sir? Are you all right, sir?'

'Yes,' I whispered. 'I'm just tired. I've come a long way.'

In the morning, I walked along the lake to the local branch of the bank and met the manager, a bird-like Indian. He confirmed that Ernest Shianyisa was the Government Chief Engineer in Kisumu, responsible for roads and supervising building and the docks, and gave me directions to his offices, a few hundred yards up from the lake shore.

'Chief Engineer is not around,' the man behind the reception desk said, without looking up.

'When will he be back?'

'Who are you?'

'I am a friend,' I said.

The man lifted his head and looked at me suspiciously from a pair of emotionless black eyes.

'Come back later.'

I spent the morning wandering around the town, breathing in the smells, looking at the faces of the people, listening to their talk. I had lunch at the hotel and then returned to the offices.

'Is Mr Shianyisa back?' I asked.

'He's out of town. Come tomorrow.'

I trudged back along the dusty roads to the hotel. Despite my exhaustion the previous night, I had not slept well. Now I lay down on my bed and slipped into unconsciousness. When I awoke, the light was softening and the lake was the colour of red wine.

'Did you find Mr Shianyisa?' the desk clerk asked.

'He was out of town.'

'Oh, yes. He is always supervising his projects here and there. But you have come all this way and you are a friend. You should go to his home. He comes home in the evening.'

'Yes,' I said. 'Perhaps.'

The delay had given me time to think for the first time since I had made my decision to come, and suddenly I doubted my sense in making this journey to Africa. What was I doing? Rushing off from my home, in middle age, to search out an old African I had not thought about for forty years. What if Ernest did not welcome me? I thought back to the last occasion on which I had seen him.

But the clerk's enthusiasm brushed my doubts aside. 'Even me, I live near him,' he said happily. 'I get off duty in half an hour. I will show you the way.'

I walked back to my room and took a shower and changed into clean clothes. I felt like a boy again. I wanted to look my best for Ernest. I was in the lobby within twenty minutes, pacing impatiently up and down. Eventually the clerk appeared and we walked to the car. Night had fallen and he directed me along the lake road and then away from the water and down a couple of unlit pot-holed lanes, and eventually up a small rise.

'You can let me off here,' he said. 'Mr Shianyisa's home is the third house on the right, with the light.'

He pointed into the night, and I followed his directions up the road and parked. The gate hung ajar and I pushed my way gently into the compound. There was a neat lawn and then a simple whitewashed bungalow. I walked up to the door and knocked.

'*Hodi,*' I whispered, the word rising from the past.

I heard footsteps, and the door half opened, and a pair of boys looked curiously up at me.

'Hello,' I said. 'I'm looking for Mr Shianyisa.'

They whispered to each other and the younger one ran off while the older boy, who must have been eight or nine, examined me through the gap. After a moment, the door opened fully and a man younger than I was, and almost as tall, looked out at me questioningly.

'I'm looking for Mr Shianyisa,' I said again.

'Yes.'

'Mr Ernest Shianyisa, the Chief Engineer.'

'Yes, that is me.'

'Oh.'

I stood there and stared at him. Then he stood aside. 'Please, come in,' he said, and he directed me to a neat, simply furnished living room. The boys followed us, but he ushered them away.

'Please sit down,' he said. 'You have come to see me?'

'Well, I thought . . . ' I looked at him again, searching for something of Ernest in his face. 'I think perhaps you are the son of the man I was expecting, a man with the same name.'

'Yes, that would be my father,' he said.

'And where is he?' I asked. I knew I was being impolite, but I could not help myself.

'My father?'

'Yes.'

'He died fifteen years ago.'

'I see,' I said, and I slumped against the back of my chair. In nearly forty years I had barely thought about Ernest, but in the past forty-eight hours I had thought about little else and now I found it hard to imagine a world, a future, without Ernest.

'Sir?' He was leaning forward and looking at me with concern in his face. 'Are you all right?'

'Sorry,' I said. 'I'm sorry about your father.'

He looked at me curiously. 'In fact,' he said slowly, 'he was not my real father. He was my adopted father. Perhaps you were his friend?'

'A long time ago,' I replied, looking back at him.

'And your name is?'

'Oh, I do apologize,' I said, shaking myself out of my reverie. 'I have forgotten myself.' I told him my name and he nodded and began to smile, and it seemed to me that I recognized this soft, shy smile, that I had seen it before.

'Please,' I said. 'May I ask your mother's name?'

'She was Mary.'

'Was?'

'She passed away. You missed her by less than a year.'

'Oh, I'm sorry, so sorry.'

'Thank you,' he said, nodding seriously. His skin was lighter than his mother's and a band of freckles was just visible across his cheeks and nose. Then he smiled again, and as he did so, I realized what he must have already realized. I understood who he was, and who I was, who we both were. I smiled back and I think we might have sat there smiling at each other for ever if one of his sons had not come to the door and told us that dinner was ready.

'You will stay, of course,' Ernest said. 'My wife is a very good cook. Please, I will let her know.'

While I waited I stood up. There were several photographs on a shelf, and one was of Mary and Ernest – Mary and the Ernest I had known, though older, in middle age. She had fattened out, but he had hardly changed. If anything he had grown even thinner and more wiry, and his face grinned out at me as I remembered it grinning from the window of the Chevrolet the very first time I saw him. Then my eye was drawn to the shelves below the photographs. They were stacked with something yellow, and bending down I saw that the yellow was the spines of hundreds of *National Geographic* magazines, neatly ordered – the complete set from 1967 to the present day.

Supper was taken up with eating and small talk. The *ugali* and meat and vegetables reminded me of the meals Margaret had cooked on the nights my parents went out, in the last year before the Trouble. When we were finished, while Mrs Shianyisa cleared the table, and the children went to bed, Ernest and I went out on to the veranda. The lake lay in front of us and the light from a moon we could not see filtered through the silver clouds and spread a pale sheen over the water.

'Mr Shianyisa –' I began.

'Please, call me Ernest,' he said. 'After all, we are brothers.'

'Yes,' I replied. 'We are brothers.'

While my father and I had been packing up and returning to England, he told me, Ernest and Mary had come to Kisumu. They had married and Mary's son had taken Ernest's name. Ernest found work as a mechanic and eventually started up his own garage, which was successful in a small way, aided, after independence, by the town's discovery that Ernest had been imprisoned during the Trouble, which made him a freedom fighter, a hero. Mary had no more children and while the old Ernest always treated the boy as his son, he told him early on about his real father in England.

The young Ernest was good at school and my father's money paid for books and uniform. The boy did not think to question this – the young take what they are given for granted – and it was only when the old Ernest died that the young Ernest tried to get in contact with his real father, with my father.

'I wrote to him through the bank,' he said. 'He never replied, but the money kept on coming. It paid for my training as an engineer. My father – Ernest, I mean – had always encouraged me to become an engineer. Now I have put away savings for my sons, as well. He is generous, your father. How is he?'

'He died six weeks ago.'

'Sorry,' he said. 'I am sorry.' Now we had both said our sorries, as if somehow on that first evening it was necessary for us to apologize for the sins of our fathers.

'Thank you,' I said.

'And now we grow old,' Ernest smiled. 'And our sons grow into men. Do you have children?'

'No,' I said. 'You see –' I was about to give him my reasons, the reasons I always gave in response to this question. But I realized that I had no reasons, that the reasons I had thought existed were no reasons at all.

We looked out into the night for a while. 'So much has changed in this country,' he said eventually. 'We forget the old ways, we are becoming Westernized. But some of our old customs survive. Perhaps you remember yourself that we do not distinguish between our children and our brothers' children. They are all our own. You are my brother and so my sons are your sons.' He turned to me and laid his hand on my shoulder. 'I would be very honoured if you would stay in our house for as long as you wish. I am happy you have come.'

'I am happy too,' I said, and as we stood looking out over the lake, I realized it was true. The moon had now finally appeared through a gap in the clouds. It wasn't a full moon, not yet, but it was getting there, and it seemed to me that it glowed with the expectation of that ripeness to come.